I0824046

VIKING MYTHS & LEGENDS

VIKING MYTHS & LEGENDS

TALES OF THE NORSE GODS

SIRIUS

This edition published in 2025 by Sirius Publishing, a division of
Arcturus Publishing Limited,
26/27 Bickels Yard, 151–153 Bermondsey Street,
London SE1 3HA

ISBN: 978-1-3988-6105-3
AD012716UK

Printed in China

Contents

Introduction

The untamed and unpredictable world of Viking mythology has intrigued readers across the globe for centuries. Gods, monsters and magical creatures have long shaped the stories of the Norsemen that have survived generations. Including exhilarating voyages, single combat, murder and vengeance, the tales inside epitomise unparalleled derring-do and extraordinary resilience.

This impressive collection of stories was originally penned by Jennie Hall and published in 1902 as *Viking Tales*. It covers the epic quest of the courageous Viking, Harald Fairhair, that takes him across oceans and perilous lands to new shores. Beginning in Harald's youth, the tales follow his life until he is crowned King of Norway and unites his people. Along the way, he faces all manner of obstacles with danger and foes lurking around every turn, from America and Greenland to Iceland and Norway.

Also included within are numerous illustrations that capture the thrill of Viking exploration, warfare and the supernatural world. Steeped in drama and adventure, the myths inside showcase these mighty seafaring warriors at their best as they overcome cunning tricksters and fearsome creatures, and achieve ultimate glory.

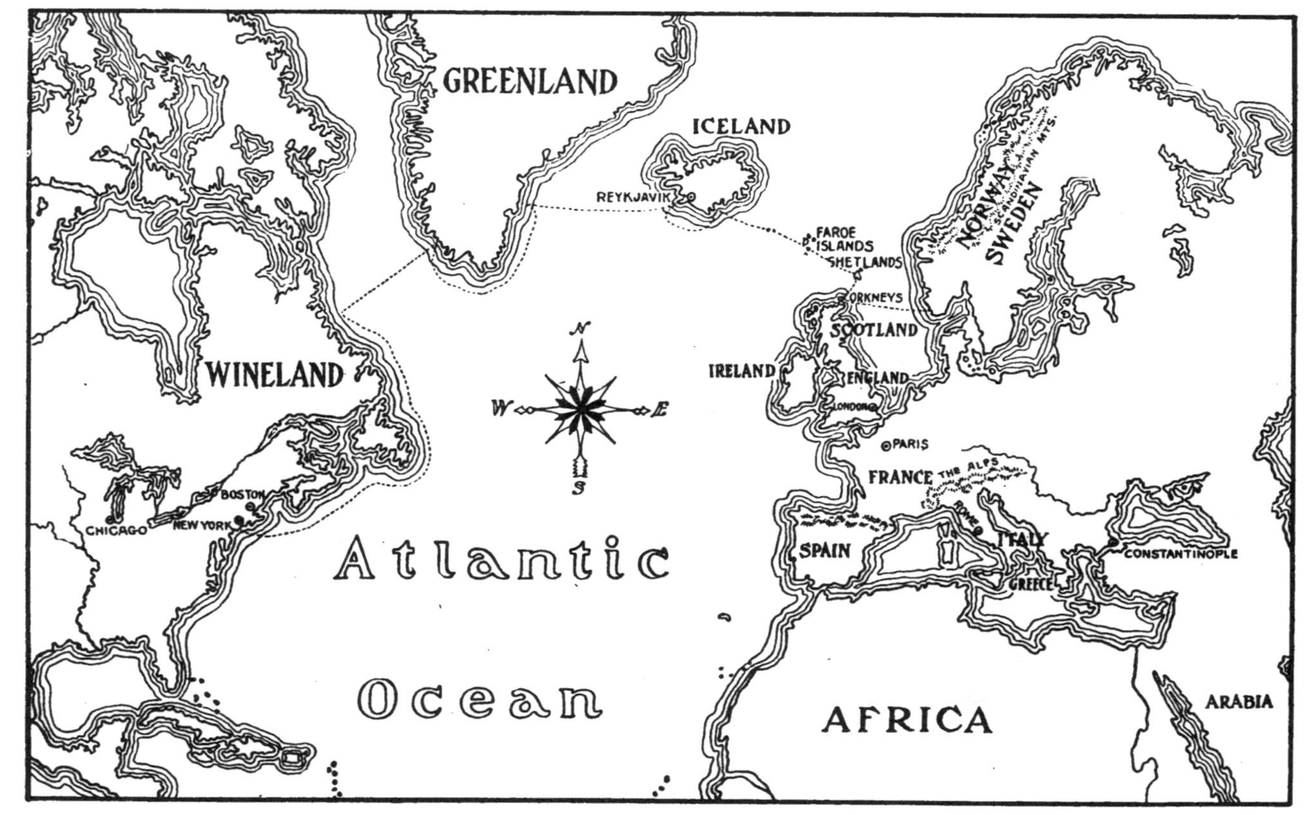

A map showing the journeys of the Vikings

The Baby

King Halfdan lived in Norway long ago. One morning his queen said to him:

'I had a strange dream last night. I thought that I stood in the grass before my bower. I pulled a thorn from my dress. As I held it in my fingers, it grew into a tall tree. The trunk was thick and red as blood, but the lower limbs were fair and green, and the highest ones were white. I thought that the branches of this great tree spread so far that they covered all Norway and even more.'

'A strange dream,' said King Halfdan. 'Dreams are the messengers of the gods. I wonder what they would tell us,' and he stroked his beard in thought.

Some time after that a serving-woman came into the feast hall where King Halfdan was. She carried a little white bundle in her arms.

'My lord,' she said, 'a little son is just born to you.'

'Ha!' cried the king, and he jumped up from the high seat and hastened forward until he stood before the woman.

'Show him to me!' he shouted, and there was joy in his voice.

The serving-woman put down her bundle on the ground and turned back the cloth. There was a little naked baby. The king looked at it carefully.

'It is a goodly youngster,' he said, and smiled. 'Bring Ivar and Thorstein.'

They were captains of the king's soldiers. Soon they came.

'Stand as witnesses,' Halfdan said.

Then he lifted the baby in his arms, while the old serving-woman brought a silver bowl of water. The king dipped his hand into it and sprinkled the baby, saying:

'I own this baby for my son. He shall be called Harald. My naming gift to him is ten pounds of gold.'

Then the woman carried the baby back to the queen's room.

'My lord owns him for his son,' she said. 'And no wonder! He is perfect in every limb.'

The queen looked at him and smiled and remembered her dream and thought:

'That great tree! Can it be this little baby of mine?'

‘I own this baby for my son. He shall be called Harald’

The Tooth Thrall

When Harald was seven months old he cut his first tooth. Then his father:

'All the young of my herds, lambs and calves and colts, that have been born since this baby was born I this day give to him. I also give to him this thrall, Olaf. These are my tooth-gifts to my son.'

The boy grew fast, for as soon as he could walk about he was out of doors most of the time. He ran in the woods and climbed the hills and waded in the creek. He was much with his tooth thrall, for the king had said to Olaf:

'Be ever at his call.'

Now this Olaf was full of stories, and Harald liked to hear them.

'Come out to Aegir's Rock, Olaf, and tell me stories,' he said almost every day.

So they started off across the hills. The man wore a long, loose coat of white wool, belted at the waist with a strap. He had on coarse shoes and leather leggings. Around his neck was an iron collar welded together so that it could not come off. On it were strange marks, called runes, that said:

'Olaf, thrall of Halfdan.'

But Harald's clothes were gay. A cape of grey velvet hung from his shoulders. It was fastened over his breast with great gold buckles. When it waved in the wind, a scarlet lining flashed out, and the bottom of a little scarlet jacket showed. His feet and legs were covered with grey woollen tights. Gold lacings wound around his legs from his shoes to his knees. A band of gold held down his long, yellow hair.

It was a wild country that these two were walking over. They were climbing steep, rough hills. Some of them seemed made all of rock, with a little earth lying in spots. Great rocks hung out from them, with trees growing in their cracks. Some big pieces had broken off and rolled down the hill.

'Thor broke them,' Olaf said. 'He rides through the sky and hurls his hammer at clouds and at mountains. That makes the thunder and the lightning and cracks the hills. His hammer never misses its aim, and it always comes back to his hand and is eager to go again.'

When they reached the top of the hill they looked back. Far below was a soft, green valley. In front of it the sea came up into the land and made a fjord. On each side of the fjord high walls of rock stood up and made the water black with shadow. All around the valley were high hills with dark pines on them. Far off were the mountains. In the valley were Halfdan's houses around their square yard.

'How little our houses look down there!' Harald said. 'But I can almost – yes, I can see the red dragon on the roof of the feast hall. Do you remember when I climbed up and sat on his head, Olaf?'

He laughed and kicked his heels and ran on.

At last they came to Aegir's Rock and walked up on its flat top.

Harald went to the edge and looked over. A ragged wall of rock reached down, and two hundred feet below was the black water of the fjord. Olaf watched him for a while, then he said:

'No whitening of your cheek, Harald? Good! A boy that can face the fall of Aegir's Rock will not be afraid to face the war flash when he is a man.'

'Ho, I am not afraid of the war flash now,' cried Harald.

He threw back his cape and drew a little dagger from his belt.

'See!' he cried; 'does this not flash like a sword? And I am not afraid. But after all, this is a baby thing! When I am eight years old I will have a sword, a sharp tooth of war.'

He swung his dagger as though it were a long sword. Then he ran and sat on a rock by Olaf.

'Why is this Aegir's Rock?' he asked.

'You know that Asgard is up in the sky,' Olaf said. 'It is a wonderful city where the golden houses of the gods are in the golden grove. A high wall runs all around it. In the house of Odin, the All-father, there is a great feast hall larger than the whole earth. Its name is Valhalla. It has five hundred doors. The rafters are spears. The roof is thatched with shields. Armour lies on the benches. In the high seat sits Odin, a golden helmet on his head, a spear in his hand. Two wolves lie at his feet. At his right hand and his left sit all the gods and goddesses, and around the hall sit thousands and thousands of men, all the brave ones that have ever died.

'Now it is good to be in Valhalla; for there is mead there better than men can brew, and it never runs out. And there are skalds that sing wonderful songs that men never heard. And before the doors of Valhalla is a great meadow where the warriors fight every day

'He threw back his cape and drew a little dagger from his belt'

and get glorious and sweet wounds and give many. And all night they feast, and their wounds heal. But none may go to Valhalla except warriors that have died bravely in battle. Men who die from sickness go with women and children and cowards to Niflheim. There Hela, who is queen, always sneers at them, and a terrible cold takes hold of their bones, and they sit down and freeze.

'Years ago Aegir was a great warrior. Aegir the Big-handed, they called him. In many a battle his sword had sung, and he had sent many warriors to Valhalla. Many swords had bit into his flesh and left marks there, but never a one had struck him to death. So his hair grew white and his arms thin. There was peace in that country then, and Aegir sorrowed, saying:

'"I am old. Battles are still. Must I die in bed like a woman? Shall I not see Valhalla?"

'Now thus did Odin say long ago:

'"If a man is old and is come near death and cannot die in fight, let him find death in some brave way and he shall feast with me in Valhalla."

'So one day Aegir came to this rock.

'"A deed to win Valhalla!" he cried.

'Then he drew his sword and flashed it over his head and held his shield high above him, and leaped out into the air and died in the water of the fjord.'

'Ho!' cried Harald, jumping to his feet. 'I think that Odin stood up before his high seat and welcomed that man gladly when he walked through the door of Valhalla.'

'So the songs say,' replied Olaf, 'for skalds still sing of that deed all over Norway.'

Olaf's Farm

At another time Harald asked:

'What is your country, Olaf? Have you always been a thrall?'

The thrall's eyes flashed.

'When you are a man,' he said, 'and go a-viking to Denmark, ask men whether they ever heard of Olaf the Crafty. There, far off, is my country, across the water. My father was Gudbrand the Big. Two hundred warriors feasted in his hall and followed him to battle. Ten sons sat at meat with him, and I was the youngest. One day he said:

'"You are all grown to be men. There is not elbow-room here for so many chiefs. The eldest of you shall have my farm when I die. The rest of you, off a-viking!"

'He had three ships. These he gave to three of my brothers. But I stayed that spring and built me a boat. I made her for only twenty oars because I thought few men would follow me; for I was young, fifteen years old. I made her in the likeness of a dragon. At the prow I carved the head with open mouth and forked tongue thrust out. I painted the eyes red for anger.

'"There, stand so!" I said, "and glare and hiss at my foes."

'In the stern I curved the tail up almost as high as the head. There I put the pilot's seat and a strong tiller for the rudder. On the breast and sides I carved the dragon's scales. Then I painted it all black and on the tip of every scale I put gold. I called her "Waverunner". There she sat on the rollers, as fair a ship as I ever saw.

'The night that it was finished I went to my father's feast. After the meats were eaten and the mead-horns came round, I stood up from my bench and raised my drinking-horn high and spoke with a great voice:

'"This is my vow: I will sail to Norway and I will harry the coast and fill my boat with riches. Then I will get me a farm and will winter in that land. Now who will follow me?"

'"He is but a boy," the men said. "He has opened his mouth wider than he can do."

'But others jumped to their feet with their mead-horns in their hands. Thirty men, one after another, raised their horns and said:

'"I will follow this lad, and I will not turn back so long as he and I live!"

'On the next morning we got into my dragon and started. I sat high in the pilot's seat. As our boat flashed down the rollers into the water I made this song and sang it:

> '"The dragon runs.
> Where will she steer?
> Where swords will sing,
> Where spears will bite,
> Where I shall laugh."

'So we harried the coast of Norway. We ate at many men's tables uninvited. Many men we found overburdened with gold. Then I said:

'"My dragon's belly is never full," and on board went the gold.

'Oh! it is better to live on the sea and let other men raise your crops and cook your meals. A house smells of smoke, a ship smells of frolic. From a house you see a sooty roof, from a ship you see Valhalla.

'Up and down the water we went to get much wealth and much frolic. After a while my men said:

'"What of the farm, Olaf?"

'"Not yet," I answered. "Viking is better for summer. When the ice comes, and our dragon cannot play, then we will get our farm and sit down."

'At last the winter came, and I said to my men:

'"Now for the farm. I have my eye on one up the coast a way in King Halfdan's country."

'So we set off for it. We landed late at night and pulled our boat up on shore and walked quietly to the house. It was rather a wealthy farm, for there were stables and a storehouse and a smithy at the sides of the house. There was but one door to the house. We went to it, and I struck it with my spear.

'"Hello! Ho! Hello!" I shouted, and my men made a great din.

'At last some one from inside said:

'"Who calls?"

'"I call," I answered. "Open! or you will think it Thor who calls," and I struck my shield against the door so that it made a great clanging.

'I struck my shield against the door so that it made a great clanging'

'The door opened only a little, but I pushed it wide and leaped into the room. It was so dark that I could see nothing but a few sparks on the hearth. I stood with my back to the wall; for I wanted no sword reaching out of the dark for me.

'"Now start up the fire," I said.

'"Come, come!" I called, when no one obeyed. "A fire! This is cold welcome for your guests."

'My men laughed.

'"Yes, a stingy host! He acts as though he had not expected us."

'But now the farmer was blowing on the coals and putting on fresh wood. Soon it blazed up, and we could see about us. We were in a little feast hall, with its fire down the middle of it. There were benches for twenty men along each side. The farmer crouched by the fire, afraid to move. On a bench in a far corner were a dozen people huddled together.

'"Ho, thralls!" I called to them. "Bring in the table. We are hungry."

'Off they ran through a door at the back of the hall. My men came in and lay down by the fire and warmed themselves, but I set two of them as guards at the door.

'"Well, friend farmer," laughed one, "why such a long face? Do you not think we shall be merry company?"

'"We came only to cheer you," said another. "What man wants to spend the winter with no guests?"

'"Ah!" another then cried out, sitting up. "Here comes something that will be a welcome guest to my stomach."

'The thralls were bringing in a great pot of meat. They set up a crane over the fire and hung the pot upon it, and we sat and watched it boil while we joked. At last the supper began. The farmer sat gloomily on the bench and would not eat, and you cannot wonder; for he saw us putting potfuls of his good beef and basket-loads of bread into our big mouths. When the tables were taken out and the mead-horns came round, I stood up and raised my horn and said to the farmer:

'"You would not eat with us. You cannot say no to half of my ale. I drink this to your health."

'Then I drank half of the hornful and sent the rest across the fire to the farmer. He took it and smiled, saying:

'"Since it is to my health, I will drink it. I thought that all this night's work would be my death."

'"Oh, do not fear that!" I laughed, "for a dead man sets no tables."

'So we drank and all grew merrier. At last I stood up and said:

'"I like this little taste of your hospitality, friend farmer. I have decided to accept more of it."

'My men roared with laughter.

'"Come," they cried, "thank him for that, farmer. Did you ever have such a lordly guest before?"

'I went on:

'"Now there is no fun in having guests unless they keep you company and make you merry. So I will give out this law: that my men shall never leave you alone. Hakon there shall be your constant companion, friend farmer. He shall not leave you day or night, whether you are working or playing or sleeping. Leif and Grim shall be the same kind of friends to your two sons."

'I named nine others and said:

'"And these shall follow your thralls in the same way. Now, am

I not careful to make your time go merrily?"

'So I set guards over every one in that house. Not once all that winter did they stir out of sight of some of us. So no tales got out to the neighbours. Besides, it was a lonely place, and by good luck no one came that way. Oh! that was fat and easy living.

'Well, after we had been there for a long time, Hakon came in to the feast one night and said:

'"I heard a cuckoo today!"

'"It is the call to go a-viking," I said.

'All my men put their hands to their mouths and shouted. Their eyes danced. Big Thorleif stood up and stretched himself.

'"I am stiff with long sitting," he said. "I itch for a fight."

'I turned to the farmer.

'"This is our last feast with you," I said.

'"Well," he laughed, "this has been the busiest winter I ever spent, and the merriest. May good luck go with you!"

'"By the beard of Odin!" I cried; "you have taken our joke like a man."

'My men pounded the table with their fists.

'"By the hammer of Thor!" shouted Grim. "Here is no stingy coward. He is a man fit to carry my drinking-horn, the horn of a sea-rover and a sword-swinger. Here, friend, take it," and he thrust it into the farmer's hand. "May you drink heart's-ease from it for many years. And with it I leave you a name, Sif the Friendly. I shall hope to drink with you sometime in Valhalla."

'Then all my men poured around that farmer and clapped him on the shoulder and piled things upon him, saying:

'"Here is a ring for Sif the Friendly."

'"And here is a bracelet."

'"A sword would not be ashamed to hang at your side."

'I took five great bracelets of gold from our treasure chest and gave them to him.

'The old man's eyes opened wide at all these things, and at the same time he laughed.

'"May Odin send me such guests every winter!" he said.

'Early next morning we shook hands with our host and boarded the "Waverunner" and sailed off.

'"Where shall we go?" my men asked.

'"Let the gods decide," I said, and tossed up my spear.

'When it fell on the deck it pointed up-shore, so I steered in that direction. That is the best way to decide, for the spear will always point somewhere, and one thing is as good as another. That time it pointed us into your father's ships. They closed in battle with us and killed my men and sunk my ship and dragged me off a prisoner. They were three against one, or they might have tasted something more bitter at our hands. They took me before King Halfdan.

'"Here," they said, "is a rascal who has been harrying our coasts. We sunk his ship and men, but him we brought to you."

'"A robber viking?" said the king, and scowled at me.

'I threw back my head and laughed.

'"Yes. And with all your fingers it took you a year to catch me."

'The king frowned more angrily.

'"Saucy, too?" he said. "Well, thieves must die. Take him out, Thorkel, and let him taste your sword."

'Your mother, the queen, was standing by. Now she put her hand on his arm and smiled and said:

'"He is only a lad. Let him live. And would he not be a good gift for our baby?"

'Your father thought a moment, then looked at your mother and smiled.

'"Soft heart!" he said gently to her; then to Thorkel, "Well, let him go, Thorkel!"

'Then he turned to me again, frowning.

'"But, young sharp-tongue, now that we have caught you we will put you into a trap that you cannot get out of. Weld an iron collar on his neck."

'So I lived and now am your tooth thrall. Well, it is the luck of war. But by the chair of Odin, I kept my vow!'

'Yes!' cried Harald, jumping to his feet. 'And had a joke into the bargain. Ah! sometime I will make a brave vow like that.'

Olaf's Fight With Havard

At another time Harald said:

'Tell me of a fight, Olaf. I want to hear about the music of swords.'

Olaf's eyes blazed.

'I will tell you of our fight with King Havard,' he said.

'One dark night we had landed at a farm. We left our "Waverunner" in the water with three men to guard her. The rest of us went into the house. The farmer met us at the door, but he died by Thorkel's sword. The others we shut into their beds. The door at each end of the hall we had barred on the inside so that nobody could surprise us. We were busy going through the cupboards and shouting at our good luck. But suddenly we heard a shout outside:

'"Thor and Havard!"

'Then there was a great beating at the doors.

'"He has two hundred fighters with him," said Grim; "for we saw his ships last night. Thirty against two hundred! We shall all drink in Valhalla tonight."

'"Well," I cried, "Odin shall have no unwilling guest in me."

'"Nor in me," cried Hakon.

'"Nor in me," shouted Thorkel.

'And that shout went all around, and we drew out our swords and caught up our shields.

'"Hot work is ahead of us," said Hakon. "Besides, we must leave none of this mead for Havard. Lend a hand, some one."

'Then he and another pulled out a great tub that sat on the floor of the cupboard.

'"I drink to Valhalla tonight," cried Thorkel the Thirsty, and he plunged his horn deep into the tub.

'When he brought it up, his sleeve was dripping and the sweet mead was running over from the horn.

'"Sloven!" cried Hakon, and he struck Thorkel with his fist and knocked him over into the cupboard.

'He fell against the wooden wall at the back, and a carved panel swung open behind him. He dropped down head first. In a minute he put his head out of the hole again. We all stood staring.

'"I think it is a secret passage," he said.

'"We will try it," I answered in a whisper. "Throw dirt on the fire. It must be dark."

'So we dug up dirt from the earth floor and smothered the fire. All this time there was a terrible shouting and hammering at the doors, but they were of heavy logs and stood.

'"I with four more will guard this door," I said, pointing to the east end.

'Immediately four men stepped to my side.

'"And I will guard the other," Hakon said, and four went with him.

'"The rest of you, down the hole!" I said. "Close the door after you. If luck is with us we will meet at the ships. Now Thor and our good swords help us! Quick! The doors are giving way."

'So we ten men stood at the doors and held back the king's soldiers. It was dark in the room, and the people out of doors could not tell how many were inside. Few were eager to be the first in.

'"Thirty swords are waiting in there to eat up the first man," we heard some one say.

'We chuckled at that.

'But the king stood in the very doorway and fought. Our five swords held him back for a long time, but at last he pushed in, and his men poured after him. We ran back and hid behind some tubs in a dark corner. The king's men went groping about and calling, but they did not find us. The room was full of shouting and running and sword-clashing; for in the dark and the noise the men could not tell their own soldiers. More than one fell by his friend's sword. When it was less crowded about the doorway, I whispered:

'"Follow me in double line. We will make for the ships. Keep close together."

'So that double line of men, with swords swinging from both sides, ran out through the dark. Swords struck out at us, and we struck back. Men ran after us shouting, but our legs were as good as theirs. But I and Hakon and one other were all that reached the ship. There we saw our "Waverunner" with sail up and bow pointing to open sea. We swam out to her and climbed aboard. Then the men swung the sail to the wind, and we moved off. Even as we went, a spear whizzed through the air, and Hakon fell dead; for the king and all his men were running to the shore.

'"After them!" they were shouting.

'Then we heard the king call to the men in his boats lying out in the water:

'"Row to shore and take us in."

'Thorkel was standing by my side. At that he laughed and said:

'"They do not answer. He left but a handful to guard his ships. They tasted our swords. And we went aboard and broke the oars and threw the sails into the water. It will be slow going for Havard tonight."

'Then he turned to the shore and sang out loudly:

> '"King Havard's ships are dead:
> Olaf's dragon flies.
> King Havard stamps the shore:
> Olaf skims the waves.
> King Havard shakes his fist.
> Olaf turns and laughs."

'That was the end of our meeting with King Havard.'

'Then he turned to the shore and sang out loudly'

Foes'-fear

Every day the boy Harald heard some such story of war or of the gods, until he could see Thor riding among the storm-clouds and throwing his hammer, until he knew that a brave man has many wounds, but never a one on his back. Many nights he dreamed that he himself walked into Valhalla, and that all the heroes stood up and shouted:

'Welcome! Harald Halfdanson!'

'Ah! the bite of the sword is sweeter than the kiss of your mother,' he said to Olaf one day. 'When shall I stand in the prow of a dragon and feast on the fight? I am hungry to see the world. Ivar the Far-goer tells me of the strange countries he has seen. Ah! we vikings are great folk. There is no water that has not licked our boats' sides. This cape of mine came in a viking boat from France. These cloak-pins came from a far country called Greece. In my father's house are golden cups from Rome, away on the southern sea. Every land pours rich things into our treasure-chest. Ivar has been to a strange country where it is all sand and is very hot. The people call their country Arabia. They have never heard of Thor or Odin. Ivar brought beautiful striped cloth from there, and wonderful, sweet-smelling waters. Oh! when shall the white horses of the sea lead me out to strange lands and glorious battles?'

But Harald did something besides listen to stories. Every morning he was up at sunrise and went with a thrall to feed the hunting dogs. Thorstein taught him to swim in the rough waters of the fjord. Often he went with the men a-hunting in the woods and learned to ride a horse and pull a bow and throw a lance. Ivar taught him to play the harp and to make up songs. He went much to the smithy, where the warriors mended their helmets and made their spears and swords of iron and bronze. At first he only watched the men or worked the bellows, but soon he could handle the tongs and hold the red-hot iron, and after a long time he learned to use the hammer and to shape metal. One day he made himself a spear-head. It was two feet long and sharp on both edges. While the iron was hot he beat into it some runes. When the men in the smithy saw the runes they opened their eyes wide and looked at the boy, for few Norsemen could read.

'What does it say?' they asked.

'It is the name of my spear-point, and it said, "Foes'-fear",' Harald said. 'But now for a handle.'

It was winter and the snow was very deep. So Harald put on his skees and started for a wood that was back from shore. Down the mountains he went, twenty, thirty feet at a slide, leaping over chasms a hundred feet across. In his scarlet cloak he looked like a flash of fire. The wind shot past him howling. His eyes danced at the fun.

'It is like flying,' he thought and laughed. 'I am an eagle. Now I soar,' as he leaped over a frozen river.

He saw a slender ash growing on top of a high rock.

'That is the handle for "Foes'-fear",' he said.

The rock stood up like a ragged tower, but he did not stop because of the steep climb. He threw off his skees and thrust his hands and feet into holes of the rock and drew himself up. He tore his jacket and cut his leather leggings and scratched his face and bruised his hands, but at last he was on the top. Soon he had chopped down the tree and had cut a straight pole ten feet long and as big around as his arm. He went down, sliding and jumping and tearing himself on the sharp stones. With a last leap he landed near his skees. As he did so a lean wolf jumped and snapped at him, snarling. Harald shouted and swung his pole. The wolf dodged, but quickly jumped again and caught the boy's arm between his sharp teeth. Harald thought of the spear-point in his belt. In a wink he had it out and was striking with it. He drove it into the wolf's neck and threw him back on the snow, dead.

'You are the first to feel the tooth of "Foes'-fear",' he said, 'but I think you will not be the last.'

Then without thinking of his torn arm he put on his skees and went leaping home. He went straight to the smithy and smoothed his pole and drove it into the haft of the spear-point. He hammered out a gold band and put it around the joining place. He made nails with beautiful heads and drove them into the pole in different places.

'If it is heavy it will strike hard,' he said.

Then he weighed the spear in his hand and found the balancing point and put another gold band there to mark it.

Thorstein came in while he was working.

'He drove it into the wolf's neck'

'A good spear,' he said.

Then he saw the torn sleeve and the red wound beneath.

'Hello!' he cried. 'Your first wound?'

'Oh, it is only a wolf-scratch,' Harald answered.

'By Thor!' cried Thorstein, 'I see that you are ready for better wounds. You bear this like a warrior.'

'I think it will not be my last,' Harald said.

Harald is King

Now when Harald was ten years old his father, King Halfdan, died. An old book that tells about Harald said that then 'he was the biggest of all men, the strongest, and the fairest to look upon'. That about a boy ten years old! But boys grew fast in those days for they were out of doors all the time, running, swimming, leaping on skees, and hunting in the forest. All that makes big, manly boys.

So now King Halfdan was dead and buried, and Harald was to be king. But first he must drink his father's funeral ale.

'Take down the gay tapestries that hang in the feast hall,' he said to the thralls. 'Put up black and grey ones. Strew the floor with pine branches. Brew twenty tubs of fresh ale and mead. Scour every dish until it shines.'

Then Harald sent messengers all over that country to his kinsmen and friends.

'Bid them come in three months' time to drink my father's funeral ale,' he said. 'Tell them that no one shall go away empty-handed.'

So in three months men came riding up at every hour. Some came in boats. But many had ridden far through mountains, swimming

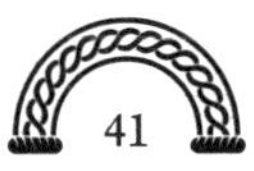

rivers; for there were few roads or bridges in Norway. On account of that hard ride no women came to the feast.

At nine o'clock in the night the feast began. The men came walking in at the west end of the hall. The great bonfires down the middle of the room were flashing light on everything. The clean smell of this wood-smoke and of the pine branches on the floor was pleasant to the guests. Down each side of the hall stretched long, backless benches, with room for three hundred men. In the middle of each side rose the high seat, a great carved chair on a platform. All along behind the benches were the black and grey draperies. Here hung the shields of the guests; for every man, when he was given his place, turned and hung his shield behind him and set his tall spear by it. So on each wall there was a long row of gay shields, red and green and yellow, and all shining with gold or bronze trimmings. And higher up there was another row of gleaming spear-points. Above the hall the rafters were carved and gaily painted, so that dragons seemed to be crawling across, or eagles seemed to be swooping down.

The guests walked in laughing and talking with their big voices so that the rafters rang. They made the hall look all the brighter with their clothes of scarlet and blue and green, with their flashing golden bracelets and head-bands and sword-scabbards, with their flying hair of red or yellow.

Across the east end of the hall was a bench. When the men were all in, the queen, Harald's mother, and the women who lived with her, walked in through the east door and sat upon this bench.

Then thralls came running in and set up the long tables before the benches. Other thralls ran in with large steaming kettles of meat. They put big pieces of this meat into platters of wood and set it before the men. They had a few dishes of silver. These they put before the guests at the middle of the tables; for the great people sat here near the high seats.

When the meat came, the talking stopped; for Norsemen ate only twice a day, and these men had had long rides and were hungry. Three or four persons ate from one platter and drank from the same big bowl of milk. They had no forks, so they ate from their fingers and threw the bones under the table among the pine branches. Sometimes they took knives from their belts to cut the meat.

When the guests sat back satisfied, Harald called to the thralls:

'Carry out the tables.'

So they did and brought in two great tubs of mead and set one at each end of the hall. Then the queen stood up and called some of her women. They went to the mead tubs. They took the horns, when the thralls had filled them, and carried them to the men with some merry word. Perhaps one woman said as she handed a man his horn:

'This horn has no feet to be set down upon. You must drink it at one draught.'

Perhaps another said:

'Mead loves a merry face.'

The women were beautiful, moving about the hall. The queen wore a trailing dress of blue velvet with long flowing sleeves. She had a short apron of striped Arabian silk with gold fringe along the bottom. From her shoulders hung a long train of scarlet wool embroidered in gold. White linen covered her head. Her long yellow hair was pulled around at the sides and over her breast and was fastened under the belt of her apron. As she walked, her train made a pleasant rustle among the pine branches. She was tall and straight and strong. Some of her younger women wore no linen on their heads and had their white arms bare, with bracelets shining on them. They, too, were tall and strong.

All the time men were calling across the fire to one another asking news or telling jokes and laughing.

An old man, Harald's uncle, sat in the high seat on the north side. That was the place of honour. But the high seat on the south side was empty; for that was the king's seat. Harald sat on the steps before it.

The feast went merrily until long after midnight. Then the thralls took some of the guests to the guest house to sleep, and some to the beds around the sides of the feast hall. But some men lay down on the benches and drew their cloaks over themselves.

On the next night there was another feast. Still Harald sat on the step before the high seat. But when the tables were gone and the horns were going around, he stood up and raised high a horn of ale and said loudly:

'This horn of memory I drink in honour of my father, Halfdan, son of Gudrod, who sits now in Valhalla. And I vow that I will grind my father's foes under my heel.'

Then he drank the ale and sat down in the king's high seat, while all the men stood up and raised their horns and shouted:

'King Harald!'

And some cried:

'That was a brave vow.'

‘I vow that I will grind my father’s foes under my heel’

And Harald's uncle called out:

'A health to King Harald!'

And they all drank it.

Then a man stood up and said:

'Hear my song of King Halfdan!' for this man was a skald.

'Yes, the song!' shouted the men, and Harald nodded his head.

So the skald took down his great harp from the wall behind him and went and stood before Harald. The bottom of the harp rested on the floor, but the top reached as high as the skald's shoulders. The brass frame shone in the light. The strings were some of gold and some of silver. The man struck them with his hand and sang of King Halfdan, of his battles, of his strong arm and good sword, of his death, and of how men loved him.

When he had finished, King Harald took a bracelet from his arm and gave it to him, saying:

'Take this as thanks for your good song.'

The guests stayed the next day and at night there was another feast.

When the mead horns were going around, King Harald stood up and spoke:

'I said that no man should go away empty-handed from drinking my father's funeral ale.'

He beckoned the thralls, and they brought in a great treasure-chest and set it down by the high seat. King Harald opened it and took out rich gifts – capes and sword-belts and beautiful cloth and bracelets and gold cloak-pins. These he sent about the hall and gave something to every man. The guests wondered at the richness of his gifts.

'This young king has an open hand,' they said, 'and deep treasure-chests.'

After breakfast the next morning the guests went out and stood by their horses ready to go, but before they mounted, thralls brought a horn of mead to each man. That was called the stirrup-horn, because after they drank it the men put their feet to the stirrups and sprang upon their horses and started. King Harald and his people rode a little way with them.

All men said that that was the richest funeral feast that ever was held.

Harald's Battle

Now King Halfdan had many foes. When he was alive they were afraid to make war upon him, for he was a mighty warrior. But when Harald became king, they said:

'He is but a lad. We will fight with him and take his land.'

So they began to make ready. King Harald heard of this and he laughed and said:

'Good! "Foes'-fear" is thirsty, and my legs are stiff with much sitting.'

He called three men to him. To one he gave an arrow, saying:

'Run and carry this arrow north. Give it into the hands of the master of the next farm, and say that all men are to meet here within two weeks from this day. They must come ready for war and mounted on horses. Say also that if a man does not obey this call, or if he receives this arrow and does not carry it on to his next neighbour, he shall be outlawed from this country, and his land shall be taken from him.'

He gave arrows to the other two men and told them to run south and east with the same message.

So all through King Harald's country men were soon busy mending helmets and polishing swords and making shields. There was blazing of forges and clanging of anvils all through the land.

On the day set, the fields about King Harald's house were full of men and horses. After breakfast a horn blew. Every man snatched his weapons and jumped upon his horse. Men of the same neighbourhood stood together, and their chief led them. They waited for the starting horn. This did not look like our army. There were no uniforms. Some men wore helmets, some did not. Some wore coats of mail, but others wore only their jackets and tights of bright-coloured wool. But at each man's left side hung a great shield. Over his right shoulder went his sword-belt and held his long sword under his left hand. Above most men's heads shone the points of their tall spears. Some men carried axes in their belts. Some carried bows and arrows. Many had ram's horns hanging from their necks.

King Harald rode at the front of his army with his standard-bearer beside him. Chain-armour covered the king's body. A red cloak was thrown over his shoulders. On his head was a gold helmet with a dragon standing up from it. He carried a round shield on his left arm. The king had made that shield himself. It was of brass. The rivets were of silver, with strangely shaped heads. On the back of Harald's horse was a red cloth trimmed with the fur of ermine.

King Harald looked up at his standard and laughed aloud.

'Oh, War-lover,' he cried, 'you and I ride out on a gay journey.'

A horn blew again and the army started. The men shouted as they went, and blew their ram's horns.

'Now we shall taste something better than even King Harald's ale,' shouted one.

Another rose in his stirrups and sniffed the air.

'Ah! I smell a battle,' he cried. 'It is sweeter than those strange waters of Arabia.'

So the army went merrily through the land. They carried no tents, they had no provision wagons.

'The sky is a good enough tent for a soldier,' said the Norsemen. 'Why carry provisions when they lie in the farms beside you?'

After two days King Harald saw another army on the hills.

'Thorstein,' he shouted, 'up with the white shield and go tell King Haki to choose his battle-field. We will wait but an hour. I am eager for the frolic.'

So Thorstein raised a white shield on his spear as a sign that he camc on an errand of peace. He rode near King Haki, but he could not wait until he came close before he shouted out his message and then turned and rode back.

'Tell your boy king that we will not hang back,' Haki called after Thorstein.

King Harald's men waited on the hillside and watched the other army across the valley. They saw King Haki point and saw twenty men ride off as he pointed. They stopped in a patch of hazel and hewed with their axes.

'They are getting the hazels,' said Thorstein.

'Audun,' said King Harald to a man near him, 'stay close to my standard all day. You must see the best of the fight. I want to hear a song about it after it is over.'

This Audun was the skald who sang at the drinking of King Halfdan's funeral ale.

King Haki's men rode down into the valley. They drove down stakes all about a great field. They tied the hazel twigs to the stakes in a string. But they left an open space toward King Harald's army and one toward King Haki's. Then a man raised a white shield and galloped toward King Harald.

'We are ready!' he shouted.

At the same time King Haki raised a red shield. King Harald's men put their shields before their mouths and shouted into them. It made a great roaring war-cry.

'Up with the war shield!' shouted King Harald. 'Horns blow!'

There was a blowing of horns on both sides. The two armies galloped down into the field and ran together. The fight had begun.

All that day long swords were flashing, spears flying, men shouting, men falling from their horses, swords clashing against shields.

'Victory flashes from that dragon,' Harald's men said, pointing to the king's helmet. 'No one stands before it.'

And, surely, before night came, King Haki fell dead under 'Foes'-fear'. When he fell, a great shout went up from his warriors, and they turned and fled. King Harald's men chased them far, but during the night came back to camp. Many brought swords and helmets and bracelets or silver-trimmed saddles and bridles with them.

'Here is what we got from the foe,' they said.

The next morning King Harald spoke to his men:

'Let us go about and find our dead.'

So they went over all the battle-field. They put every man on

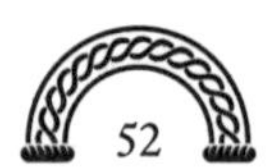

"King Haki fell dead under 'Foe's-fear'"

his shield and carried him and laid him on a hill-top. They hung his sword over his shoulder and laid his spear by his side. So they laid all the dead together there on the hill-top. Then King Harald said, looking about:

'This is a good place to lie. It looks far over the country. The sound of the sea reaches it. The wind sweeps here. It is a good grave for Norsemen and Vikings. But it is a long road and a rough road to Valhalla that these men must travel. Let the nearest kinsman of each man come and tie on his hell-shoes. Tie them fast, for they will need them much on that hard road.'

So friends tied shoes on the dead men's feet. Then King Harald said:

'Now let us make the mound.'

Every man set to work with what tools he had and heaped earth over the dead until a great mound stood up. They piled stones on the top. On one of these stones King Harald made runes telling how these men had died.

After that was done King Harald said:

'Now set up the pole, Thorstein. Let every man bring to that pole all that he took from the foe.'

So they did, and there was a great hill of things around it. Harald divided it into piles.

'This pile we will give to Thor in thanks for the victory,' he said. 'This pile is mine because I am king. Here are the piles for the chiefs, and these things go to the other men of the army.'

So every man went away from that battle richer than he was before, and Thor looked down from Valhalla upon his full temple and was pleased.

The next morning King Harald led his army back. But on the way he met other foes and had many battles and did not lose one. The kings either died in battle or ran away, and Harald had their lands.

'He has kept his vow,' men said, 'and ground his father's foes under his heel.'

So King Harald sat in peace for a while.

Gyda's Saucy Message

Now Harald heard men talk of Gyda, the daughter of King Eric.

'She is very beautiful,' they said, 'but she is very proud, too. She can both read and make runes. No other woman in the world knows so much about herbs as she does. She can cure any sickness. And she is proud of all this!'

Now when King Harald heard that, he thought to himself:

'Fair and proud. I like them both. I will have her for my wife.'

So he called his uncle, Guthorm, and said:

'Take rich gifts and go to Gyda's foster-father and tell him that I will marry Gyda.'

So Guthorm and his men came to that house and they told the king's message to the foster-father. Gyda was standing near, weaving a rich cloak. She heard the speech. She came up and said, holding her head high and curling her lip:

'I will not waste myself on a king of so few people. Norway is a strange country. There is a little king here and a little king there – hundreds of them scattered about. Now in Denmark there is but one great king over the whole land. And it is so in Sweden. Is no one brave enough to make all of Norway his own?'

She laughed a scornful laugh and walked away. The men stood with open mouths and stared after her. Could it be that she had sent that saucy message to King Harald? They looked at her foster-father. He was chuckling in his beard and said nothing to them. They started out of the house in anger. When they were at the door, Gyda came up to them again and said:

'Give this message to your King Harald for me: I will not be his wife unless he puts all of Norway under him for my sake.'

So Guthorm and his men rode homeward across the country. They did not talk. They were all thinking. At last one said:

'How shall we give this message to the king?'

'I have been thinking of that,' Guthorm said; 'his anger is no little thing.'

It was late when they rode into the king's yard; for they had ridden slowly, trying to make some plan for softening the message, but they had thought of none.

'I see light through the wind's-eyes of the feast hall,' one said.

'Yes, the king keeps feast,' Guthorm said. 'We must give our message before all his guests.'

So they went in with very heavy hearts. There sat King Harald in the high seat. The benches on both sides were full of men. The tables had been taken out, and the mead-horns were going round.

'Oh, ho!' cried King Harald. 'Our messengers! What news?'

Then Guthorm said:

'This Gyda is a bold and saucy girl, King Harald. My tongue refuses to give her message.'

The king stamped his foot.

'Out with it!' he cried. 'What does she say?'

'I will not be his wife unless he puts all of Norway under him for my sake'

'She says that she will not marry so little a king,' Guthorm answered.

Harald jumped to his feet. His face flushed red. Guthorm stretched out his hand.

'They are not my words, O King; they are the words of a silly girl.'

'Is there any more?' the king shouted. 'Go on!'

'She said: "There is one king in Denmark and one king in Sweden. Is there no man brave enough to make himself king of all Norway? Tell King Harald that I will not marry him unless he puts all of Norway under him for my sake."'

The guests sat speechless, staring at Guthorm. All at once the king broke into a roar of laughter.

'By the hammer of Thor!' he cried, 'that is a good message. I thank you, Gyda. Did you hear it, friends? King of all Norway! Why, we are all stupids. Why did we not think of that?'

Then he raised his horn high.

'Now hear my vow. I say that I will not cut my hair or comb it until I am king of all Norway. That I will be or I will die.'

Then he drank off the horn of mead, and while he drank it, all the men in the hall stood up and waved their swords and shouted and shouted. That old hall in all its two hundred years of feasts had not heard such a noise before.

'Ah, Harald!' Guthorm cried, 'surely Thor in Valhalla smiled when he heard that vow.'

The men sat all night talking of that wonderful vow.

On the very next day King Harald sent out his war-arrows. Soon a great army was gathered. They marched through the country north and south and east and west, burning houses and fighting

battles as they went. People fled before them, some to their own kings, some inland to the deep woods and hid there. But some went to King Harald and said:

'We will be your men.'

'Then take the oath, and I will be friends with you,' he said.

The men took off their swords and laid them down and came one by one and knelt before the king. They put their heads between his knees and said:

'From this day, Harald Halfdanson, I am your man. I will serve you in war. For my land I will pay you taxes. I will be faithful to you as my king.'

Then Harald said:

'I am your king, and I will be faithful to you.'

Many kings took that oath and thousands of common men. Of all the battles that Harald fought, he did not lose one.

Now for a long time the king's hair and beard had not been combed or cut. They stood out around his head in a great bushy mat of yellow. At a feast one day when the jokes were going round, Harald's uncle said:

'Harald, I will give you a new name. After this you shall be called Harald Shockhead. As my naming gift I give you this drinking-horn.'

'It is a good name,' laughed all the men.

After that all people called him Harald Shockhead.

During these wars, whenever King Harald got a country for his own, this is what he did. He said:

'All the marshland and the woodland where no people live is mine. For his farm every man shall pay me taxes.'

Over every country he put some brave, wise man and called him jarl. He said to the jarls:

'You shall collect the taxes and pay them to me. But some you shall keep for yourselves. You shall punish any man who steals or murders or does any wicked thing. When your people are in trouble they shall come to you, and you shall set the thing right. You must keep peace in the land. I will not have my people troubled with robber vikings.'

The jarls did all these things as best they could; for they were good strong men. The farmers were happy. They said:

'We can work on our farms with peace now. Before King Harald came, something was always wrong. The vikings would come and steal our gold and our grain and burn our houses, or the king would call us to war. Those little kings are always fighting. It is better under King Harald.'

But the chiefs, who liked to fight and go a-viking, hated King Harald and his new ways. One of these chiefs was Solfi. He was a king's son. Harald had killed his father in battle. Solfi had been in that battle. At the end of it he fled away with two hundred men and got into ships.

'We will make that Shockhead smart,' he said.

So they harried the coast of King Harald's country. They filled their ships with gold. They ate other men's meals. They burned farmhouses behind them. The people cried out to the jarls for help. So the jarls had out their ships all the time trying to catch Solfi, but he was too clever for them.

In the spring he went to a certain king, Audbiorn, and said to him:

'Now, there are two things that we can do. We can become this Shockhead Harald's thralls, we can kneel before him and put our heads between his knees. Or else we can fight. My father thought it better to die in battle than to be any man's thrall. How is it? Will you join with my cousin Arnvid and me against this young Shockhead?'

'Yes, I will do it,' said the king.

The Sea Fight

Many men felt as Solfi did. So when King Audbiorn and King Arnvid sent out their war arrows, a great host gathered. All men came by sea. Two hundred ships lay at anchor in the fjord, looking like strange swimming animals because of their high carved prows and bright paint. There were red and gold dragons with long necks and curved tails. Sea-horses reared out of the water. Green and gold snakes coiled up. Sea-hawks sat with spread wings ready to fly. And among all these curved necks stood up the tall, straight masts with the long yardarms swinging across them holding the looped-up sails.

When the starting horn blew, and their sails were let down, it was like the spreading of hundreds of curious flags. Some were striped black and yellow or blue and gold. Some were white with a black raven or a brown bear embroidered on them, or blue with a white sea-hawk, or black with a gold sun. Some were edged with fur. As the wind filled the gaudy sails, and the ships moved off, the men waved their hands to the women on shore and sang:

'To the sea! To the sea!
The wind in our sail,
The sea in our face,
And the smell of the fight.
After ship meets ship,
In the quarrel of swords
King Harald shall lie
In the caves under sea
And Norsemen shall laugh.'

In the prow stood men leaning forward and sniffing the salt air with joy. Some were talking of King Harald.

'Yesterday he had a hard fight,' they said. 'Today he will be lying still, dressing his wounds and mending his ships. We shall take him by surprise.'

They sailed near the coast. Solfi in his 'Sea-hawk' was ahead leading the way. Suddenly men saw his sail veer and his oars flash out. He had quickly turned his boat and was rowing back. He came close to King Arnvid and called:

'He is there, ahead. His boats are ready in line of battle. The fox has not been asleep.'

King Arnvid blew his horn. Slowly his boats came into line with his 'Sea-stag' in the middle. Again he blew his horn. Cables were thrown across from one prow to the next, and all the ships were tied together so that their sides touched. Then the men set their sails again and they went past a tongue of land into a broad fjord. There lay the long line of King Harald's ships with their fierce heads grinning and mocking at the newcomers. Back of those prows was what looked like a long wall with spots of green and red and blue and yellow and shining gold. It was the locked shields of the men in the bows, and over every shield looked fierce blue eyes. Higher up and farther back was another wall of shields; for on the half deck in the stern of every ship stood the captain with his shield-guard of a dozen men.

Arnvid's people had furled their sails and were taking down the masts, but the ships were still drifting on with the wind. The horn blew, and quickly every man sprang to his place in bow and stern. All were leaning forward with clenched teeth and widespread nostrils. They were clutching their naked swords in their hands. Their flashing eyes looked over their shields.

Soon King Arnvid's ships crashed into Harald's line, and immediately the men in the bows began to swing their swords at one another. The soldiers of the shield-guard on the high decks began to throw darts and stones and to shoot arrows into the ships opposite them.

So in every ship showers of stones and arrows were falling, and many men died under them or got broken arms or legs. Spears were hurled from deck to deck and many of them bit deep into men's bodies. In every bow men slashed with their swords at the foes in the opposite ship. Some jumped upon the gunwale to get nearer or hung from the prow-head. Some even leaped into the enemy's boat.

King Harald's ship lay prow to prow with King Arnvid's. The battle had been going on for an hour. King Harald was still in the stern on the deck. There was a dent in his helmet where a great stone had struck. There was a gash in his shoulder where a spear had cut. But he was still fighting and laughed as he worked.

'Wolf meets wolf today,' he said. 'But things are going badly in the prow,' he cried. 'Ivar fallen, Thorstein wounded, a dozen men lying in the bottom of the boat!'

He leaped down from the deck and ran along the gunwale, shouting as he went:

'Harald and victory!'

So he came to the bow and stood swinging his sword as fast as he breathed. Every time it hit a man of Arnvid's men. Harald's own warriors cheered, seeing him.

'Harald and victory!' they shouted, and went to work again with good heart.

Slowly King Arnvid's men fell back before Harald's biting sword. Then Harald's men threw a great hook into that boat and pulled it alongside and still pushed King Arnvid's people back.

'Come on! Follow me!' cried Harald.

Then he leaped into King Arnvid's boat, and his warriors followed him.

'He comes like a mad wolf,' King Arnvid's men said, and they turned and ran back below the deck.

Then Arnvid himself leaped down and stood with his sword raised.

'Can this young Shockhead make cowards of you all?' he cried.

But Harald's sword struck him, and he fell dead. Then a big, bloody viking of King Arnvid leaped upon the edge of the ship and stood there. He held his drinking-horn and his sword high in his hands.

'Rán and not you, Shockhead, shall have them and me!' he cried, and leaped laughing into the water and was drowned.

‘Then he leaped into King Arnvid’s boat’

Many other warriors chose the same death on that terrible day.

All along the line of boats men fought for hours. In some places the cables had been cut, and the boats had drifted apart. Ships lay scattered about two by two, fighting. Many boats sank, many men died, some fled away in their ships, and at the end King Harald had won the battle. So he had King Arnvid's country and King Audbiorn's country. Many men took the oath and became his friends. All people were talking of his wonderful battles.

King Harald's Wedding

It had taken King Harald ten years to fight so many battles. And all that time he had not cut his hair or combed it. Now he was feasting one day at a jarl's house. Many people were there.

'How is it, friends?' Harald said. 'Have I kept my vow?'

His friends answered:

'You have kept your vow. There is no king but you in all Norway.'

'Then I think I will cut my hair,' the king laughed.

So he went and bathed and put on fresh clothes. Then the jarl cut his hair and beard and combed them and put a gold band about his head. Then he looked at him and said:

'It is beautiful, smooth, and yellow.'

And all people wondered at the beauty of the king's hair.

'I will give you a new name,' the jarl said. 'You shall no longer be called Shockhead. You shall be called Harald Hairfair.'

'It is a good name,' everybody cried.

Then Harald said:

'But I have another thing to do now. Guthorm, you shall take the same message to Gyda that you gave ten years ago.'

So Guthorm went and brought back this answer from Gyda:

'I will marry the king of all Norway.'

So when the wedding time came, Harald rode across the country to the home of Gyda's father, Eric. Many men followed him. They were all richly dressed in velvet and gold.

For three nights they feasted at Eric's house. On the next night Gyda sat on the cross-bench with her women. A long veil of white linen covered her face and head and hung down to the ground. After the mead-horns had been brought in, Eric stood up from his high seat and went down and stood before King Harald.

'Will you marry Gyda now?' he asked.

Harald jumped to his feet and laughed.

'Yes,' he said. 'I have waited long enough.'

Then he stepped down from his high seat and stood by Eric. They walked about the hall. Before them walked thralls carrying candles. Behind them walked many of King Harald's great jarls. Three times they walked around the hall. The third time they stopped before the cross-bench. King Harald and Eric stepped upon the platform, where the cross-bench was.

Eric gave a holy hammer to Harald, and it was like the hammer of Thor.

Harald put it upon Gyda's lap, saying:

'With this holy hammer of Thor's, I, Harald, King of Norway, take you, Gyda, for my wife.'

Then he took a bunch of keys and tied it to Gyda's girdle, saying:

'This is the sign that you are mistress of my house.'

After that, Eric called out loudly:

'Now, are Harald, King of Norway, and Gyda, daughter of Eric,

'I, Harald, King of Norway, take you, Gyda, for my wife'

man and wife.'

Then thralls brought meat and drink in golden dishes. They were about to serve it to Gyda for the bride's feast, but Harald took the dish from them and said:

'No, I will serve my bride.'

So he knelt and held the platter. When he did that his men shouted. Then they talked among themselves, saying:

'Surely Harald never knelt before. It is always other people who kneel to him.'

When the bride had tasted the food and touched the mead-horn to her lips she stood up and walked from the hall. All her women followed her, but the men stayed and feasted long.

On the next morning at breakfast Gyda sat by Harald's side. Soon the king rose and said:

'Father-in-law, our horses stand ready in the yard. Work is waiting for me at home and on the sea. Lead out the bride.'

So Eric took Gyda by the hand and led her out of the hall. Harald followed close. When they passed through the door Eric said:

'With this hand I lead my daughter out of my house and give her to you, Harald, son of Halfdan, to be your wife. May all the gods make you happy!'

Harald led his bride to the horse and lifted her up and set her behind his saddle and said:

'Now this Gyda is my wife.'

Then they drank the stirrup-horn and rode off.

'Everything comes to King Harald,' his men said; 'wife and land and crown and victory in battle. He is a lucky man.'

King Harald Goes West-Over-Seas

Now many men hated King Harald. Many a man said:

'Why should he put himself up for king of all of us? He is no better than I am. Am I not a king's son as well as he? And are not many of us kings' sons? I will not kneel before him and promise to be his man. I will not pay him taxes. I will not have his jarl sitting over me. The good old days have gone. This Norway has become a prison. I will go away and find some other place.'

So hundreds of men sailed away. Some went to France and got land and lived there. Big Rolf-go-afoot and all his men sailed up the great French River and won a battle against the French king himself. There was no way to stop the flashing of his battle-axes but to give him what he wanted. So the king made Rolf a duke, gave him broad lands and gave him the king's own daughter for wife. Rolf called his country Normandy, for old Norway. He ruled it well and was a great lord, and his sons' sons after him were kings of England.

Other Norsemen went to Ireland and England and Scotland. They drew up their boats on the river banks. The people ran away before them and gathered into great armies that marched

back to meet the vikings in battle. Sometimes the Norsemen lost, but oftener they won, so that they got land and lived in those countries. Their houses sat in these strange lands like warriors' camps, and the Norsemen went among their new neighbours with hanging swords and spears in hand, ever ready for fight.

There are many islands north of Scotland. They are called the Orkneys and the Shetlands. They have many good harbours for ships. They are little and rocky and bare of trees. Wild sea-birds scream around them. On some of them a man can stand in the middle and see the ocean all about him. Now the vikings sailed to these islands and were pleased.

'It is like being always in a boat,' they said. 'This shall be our home.'

So it went until all the lands round about were covered with vikings. Norse carved and painted houses brightened the hillsides. Viking ships sailed all the seas and made harbour in every river. Norsemen's thralls ploughed the soil and planted crops and herded cattle, and gold flowed into their masters' treasure-chests. Norse warriors walked up and down the land, and no man dared to say them nay.

These men did not forget Norway. In the summers they sailed back there and harried the coast. They took gold and grain and beautiful cloth back to their homes. In Norway they left burning houses and weeping women.

Every summer King Harald had out his ships and men and hunted these vikings. There are many little islands about Norway. They have crags and caves and deep woods. Here the vikings hid when they saw King Harald's ships coming. But Harald ran his

'In Norway they left burning houses and weeping women'

boat into every creek and fjord and hunted in every cave and through all the woods and among the crags. He caught many men, but most of them got away and went home laughing at Harald. Then they came back the next summer and did the same deeds over again. At last King Harald said:

'There is but one thing to do. I must sail to these western islands and whip these robbers in their own homes.'

So he went with a great number of ships. He found as brave men as he had brought from Norway. These vikings had brought their old courage to their new homes. King Harald's fine ships were scarred by viking stones and scorched by viking fire. The shields of Harald's warriors had dents from viking blows. Many of those men carried viking scars all their lives. And many of King Harald's warriors walked the long, hard road to Valhalla, and feasted there with some of these very vikings that had died in King Harald's battles. But after many hard fights on land and sea, after many men had died and many had fled away to other lands, King Harald won, and he made the men that were yet in the islands take the oath, and he left his jarls to rule over them. Then he went back to Norway.

'He has done more than he vowed to do,' people said. 'He has not only whipped the vikings, but he has got a new kingdom west-over-seas.'

Then they talked of that dream that his mother had.

'King Harald was that great tree,' they said. 'The trunk was red with the blood of his many battles, but higher up the limbs were fair and green like this good time of peace. The topmost branches were white because Harald will live to be an old man.

Just as that tree spread out until all of Norway was in its shade, and even more lands, so Harald is king of all this country and of the western islands. The many branches of that tree are the many sons of Harald, who shall be jarls and kings in Norway, and their sons after them, for hundreds of years.'

Homes in Iceland

Men had been feasting in Ingolf's house. But there was no laughing and no shouting of jokes. Ingolf sat in his high seat frowning and gloomy. His head hung on his breast. He was staring into the fire. Now he raised his head and looked about the hall.

'Comrades,' he said, 'what shall we do? Herstein and Holmstein died by our swords. Their kinsmen hunger to kill us. Besides, when Harald hears of our deed, there will not be a safe place in Norway for us. He will never let a man fight out an honest quarrel. Where shall we go?'

A man stood up from the bench.

'We have friends in the Shetlands,' he said. 'Let us find homes there.'

Then Leif, in the high seat opposite Ingolf, stood up.

'No, not the Shetlands, my foster-brother. They are crowded already. Besides, Harald will not long keep his hands off them. Then they will be no better than Norway. England and Ireland and Scotland are old. My eyes ache for something new. What of that far island that Floki found? It is empty. We could choose

our land from the whole country. There is good fishing. There are green valleys. And Butter Thorolf says that butter drops from every weed. There are mountains and deserts where we may find adventure. I say, let us steer for Iceland!'

When he stopped, many of the men shouted:

'Yes! Iceland!'

But an old man stood up.

'We have all laughed at that tale of Butter Thorolf's,' he said. 'But Floki himself said that the sea about the island is full of ice that pushes upon the land, that no ship can live in that water in the winter, that great mountains of ice cover the island. Did not all his cattle die there of hunger and cold, and did he not come back to Norway cursing Iceland?'

'Oh, Sighvat, you are old and fearful,' called out Leif, and he laughed.

Then he stretched himself up and threw back his head.

'Are we afraid of ice? Have we not seen angry water before? I have been hungry, but I have never died of it. Surely if there are fish in the sea and grass in the valleys, we can live there. I should like to stand on a hill and look around on a wide land and think, "This is all ours," and out upon a rough sea and think, "Far off there are our foes and they dare not come over to us." Besides, we shall have no Shockhead Harald to lord it over us. We can come and go and feast and fight as we please. We shall be our own kings. And our ships will be always waiting to take us away, when we are weary of it. And we shall see things that other men have never seen. I am tired of the old things. Perhaps in after days men will make songs about "those foster-brothers, Ingolf and Leif, who made a new country in a wonderful land, and whose sons and grandsons are mighty men in Iceland!"'

Ingolf leaped up from his chair.

'By the strong arm of Thor!' he cried, 'I like the sound of it. Now I make my vow.'

He raised his drinking-horn.

'I vow that I will find this Iceland and pass the winter there, and that if man can live upon it I will go back there and set up my home.'

'And I vow that I will follow my foster-brother,' cried Leif.

And many men vowed to go.

So on the next day they began to make ready a boat. They looked her over carefully and recaulked every seam and freshly painted her and put into her their strongest oars and made her a new sail.

'This will be the longest voyage that she ever made,' Ingolf said.

When the work was done, they put into her great stores, axes, hammers, fish-nets, cooking-kettles, kegs of ale, chests of hard bread, chests of smoked meat, brass kettles full of flour, skin bottles of water. They stowed these things away in the ends of the ship. When they were ready they put in four head of cattle.

'We shall need the milk and perhaps the meat,' Ingolf said.

Many men wished to go, but Ingolf had said:

'There is little room to spare and little food and drink. I have planned for half a year. But perhaps we must be sailing longer than that. Our food may run short. We must not have extra mouths to feed. There are thirty oars in our boat. I will take only one man for every oar, and Leif and I will steer.'

So they started off. Leif stood in the prow leaning forward and looking far ahead, and he sang:

'What does the swimming dragon smell?
A stormy sea, an empty land,
Hunger, darkness, giants, fire.
Leif and his sword do laugh at that.'

They sailed for days and saw no land. Sometimes they passed ships and always made sure to sail close enough to hail them.

'Where are you going?' Ingolf would call.

'To Norway,' would come back the answer.

'For trade or fight?' Leif would shout.

Then would ring out a great laugh from that boat and this answer:

'A shut mouth is a good friend.'

So the two ships sailed on, and the men were glad to have heard a greeting and to have called one.

But at last there were the Shetlands.

'We will go in here and rest,' Ingolf said.

When they rowed to shore a certain Shetland man stood there. He watched them land and looked them all over. Then he walked up to Ingolf and said:

'You look like brave men. Welcome to Shetland. You shall come to my house and rest your legs from ship-going and fill your stomachs. I hunger for news of Norway.'

So they went to his house and stayed there for three days. And good it seemed to be near a fire and in a quiet bed and before a steaming platter. When they went to the shore to start off again, the Shetland man had his thralls carry a keg of ale and a great kettle of cooked meat and put them into the ship.

'Think of me when you eat this,' he said.

Then the Norsemen put to sea again and sailed for a long time.

One day a terrible storm came up; the sky was black; the wind howled through the ship. Great waves leaped in the sea.

'Down with the sail and out with the oars!' Ingolf shouted.

So the men furled the sail and took down the mast and laid it along the bottom of the boat. As they worked, one man was washed overboard and drowned. The men sat down to row, but the tumbling waves tossed the boat about and poured over her and broke three of the oars. But still the men held on. They were wet to the skin and were cold, and their arms and legs ached with the hard work, and they were hungry from the long waiting, but not one face was white with fear.

'Rán, in her caves under sea, wants us for company tonight,' Ingolf laughed.

So they tossed about all night, but in the morning the wind died down. Great waves still rolled, and for days the sea was rough, but they could put up the sail. Then one day Leif, as he sat in the pilot's seat, jumped to his feet and sang:

'To eyes grown tired with looking far,
All at once appeared an island,
A stretching-place for sea-legs,
A quiet bed for backs grown stiff
On rowing-bench on rolling sea.

A place to build a red fire
And thaw the blood that sea-winds froze.'

But when they came near they saw no place to land. The island was like a mountain of rock standing out of the water. The sides were steep and smooth. They sailed around it, but found no place to climb up.

'There are many other islands here,' said Leif. 'We will try another.'

So he steered to another. It, too, was a steep rock, but one side sloped down to the water and was green with grass.

'Oh, I have not seen anything so good as that green grass since I looked into my mother's face,' one man said.

There was a little harbour there. The men rowed in and quickly jumped out and put the rollers under the ship and pulled her upon shore. Then they threw themselves down on the grass and rolled and stretched their arms and shouted for joy. After that they built a fire and warmed themselves and cooked a meal and ate like wolves. They slept there that night.

In the morning before Ingolf's men started away they were standing high up on the hillside, looking about. They saw no houses on any of the islands, but they saw smoke rise from one hillside.

'Some other men, like us, weary of the sea and stopping to rest,' said Ingolf.

They saw the island that they had sailed around the night before.

'There can surely be nothing but birds' nests on top of that,' Sighvat said.

'Look!' cried another, pointing.

Men were standing on the flat top of that island. They were letting a boat down the steep side with ropes. When it struck the water, they made a rope fast to the rock and slid down it into the ship and sailed off.

'Some robber vikings from Scotland or Ireland,' laughed Leif. 'It is a good hiding place for treasure.'

Soon Ingolf and his men got into their ship and were off. Old Sighvat grumbled.

'Is this land not new enough and empty enough and far enough? I am tired of sea, sea, sea, and nothing else.'

'We started for Iceland,' said Ingolf, 'and I will not stop before I come there. I have a vow. Did you make none, Sighvat?'

Then they were on the water again for weeks with no sight of land.

'Oh! I would give my right hand to see a dragon pawing the water off there and to fling a word to its men,' Sighvat said.

'No hope of that,' replied Ingolf. 'Only three dragons before ours have ever swept this water, and men are not sailing this way for pleasure or riches.'

So only the desolate sea stretched around them. Sometimes it was smooth and shining under the sun. Often it was torn by winds, and a grey sky hung over it, and the men were drenched with rain. Once they ran into a fog. For three days and nights they could not see sun or stars to steer by. They forgot which way was north. When after three days the fog lifted, they found that they had been going in the wrong direction, and they had to turn around and sail all that weary way over again. But at last one afternoon they saw a white cloud resting on the water far off. As they sailed toward it, it grew into long stretches of black, hilly shore with a blue ice mountain rising from it. The sun was going down behind that mountain, and long lines of pink and of shining green, and great purple shadows streaked the blue.

'It is Iceland!' shouted the men.

'It is like Asgard the Shining,' Ingolf said.

But it was still far off. Men can see a long way there because the air is so clear. So Ingolf and his people sailed on for hours and at last came into a harbour. A little green valley sloped up from it. On one side was the bright ice mountain. Back of it were bare black and red hills. In that valley Ingolf and his men drew up their boat and camped. At supper that night one of the men said:

'I almost think I never felt a fire before or had warm food in my mouth.'

The men laughed.

'It is four months since we left Norway,' Ingolf said. 'Few men have ever been on the sea so long.'

That night they put up the awning in the boat and slept under it.

After that some men went fishing every day in the rowboat that they had. And Ingolf took others, and they sailed along the shore, seeing what kind of a land this was. But winter began to come on. Then Ingolf said:

'Remember what Floki said of the ice and the rough sea in winter. Soon we cannot sail any longer. Let us choose a place to stay and build a hut there and cut hay for our cattle.'

So they did. Their hut was a little mean thing of stones and turf. They kept the cattle and the hay in it. Sometimes they slept

there, when it was very cold. But most of the time they ate and slept by a great bonfire out of doors where it was clean. Leif said:

'I like the cold air of the sea better than the bad-smelling air of a house, even though it is warm.'

Now every day Ingolf and Leif and some of the men walked about the island. At night they all sat around the campfire and talked of what they had seen during the day.

'This is surely a wonderful land,' Ingolf said once. 'It is at the same time like Niflheim and like Asgard. Here is a spot green and soft, a sweet cradle for men. Next it is a mountain of ice where men would freeze to death. And next to that is a hill of rock that seems to have come out of some great fire. Yesterday I saw a cave on the seashore. The door of it was big enough for a giant. The waves broke at the doorstep. A terrible roaring came from the cave. I think it is the home of a giant. I think that giants of fire and giants of frost made this island. I have seen great basins in the rocks filled with warm water. They looked like giants' bath-tubs. I have seen boiling water shoot up out of the ground. I have walked, and have felt and heard a great rumbling under me as though some giant were sleeping there and turning over in his sleep. One day I stood on a mountain and looked inland. There was a wide desert of sand and black and red rock with nothing growing on it. The fierce wind blew dirt into my eyes, and the cold of it froze the marrow in my bones. When I have seen these things I have cursed the country, and have said: "The gods hate Iceland. I will not stay here." But then I have walked through beautiful warm valleys where the winds did not come. I saw in my mind the flowers that we found last summer. I saw our cattle feeding on the sweet grass. I thought of the sea full of good fish. I saw my house built among green fields, and my wife sitting in her home, and my children playing among the flowers and making up tales about the bright ice mountains. I saw the wide, rough seas between me and Harald and our foes. Then I thought to myself, "It is the sweetest home on earth." As for me, I am coming here to live. What do you say, comrades?'

'Have I not vowed to follow you, foster-brother?' said Leif. 'And indeed I never saw a land that I liked better. I don't believe in your giants. My sword is my god, and my ship is my temple, and I like this land to set them up in.'

They sat about the fire long that night making plans.

'You shall go home and get our women and our things, Ingolf,' said Leif. 'I will off to Ireland and have a frolic. There will be little play of swords in this empty land, and I want to have one last game before I hang up my battle-knife. Besides, I will come to you with a ship full of gold and clothes and house-hangings such as we cannot get here, and they will cost me nothing but the swing of a sword.'

As they talked, Ingolf looked up at the sky. The northern lights were quivering there. They were like great flames of yellow and green and red.

'See,' he said, and pointed. 'We are not so far that the gods will forget us. There is the flash of the armour of the Valkyrias. A battle is on somewhere, and Odin has sent his maidens to choose the heroes for Valhalla.'

Leif only laughed and lay down to sleep.

So in the spring they all went back to Norway. Leif got ready the boat again and merrily sailed for Ireland.

'Here I go to get riches for our new land,' he said.

Ingolf set his men to cutting down pines in the forest and some to building a new ship. He had his thralls plant large crops of grain and grind flour and make new kegs and chests of wood. He himself worked much at the forge, making all kinds of tools – spades, axes, hammers, hunting-knives, cooking kettles. The women were busy weaving and sewing new clothes. Ingolf sold his house and land and everything that he could not take with him.

After about two years Leif came back. He had ten thralls that he had got in Ireland. He took Ingolf aboard his ship and raised the covers of great chests. Gold helmets, silver-trimmed drinking-horns, embroidered robes, and swords flashed out.

'Did I not say that I would come back with a full ship?' he laughed.

At last all things were ready for starting.

'Today I will sacrifice to Thor and Odin,' Ingolf said. 'If the omens are good we will start tomorrow.'

'Well, go, foster-brother,' laughed Leif. 'But I have better things to do. I will be putting the cattle into the ship and will have all ready.'

So Ingolf and his men went into the forests a little way. There in a cleared space stood a large building. In front of this temple the men killed two horses for Odin. Ingolf caught some of the blood in a brass bowl. He raised it and looked up at the sky and said:

'All-wise and all-father Odin, and Thor who loves the thunder, I give these horses to you. Tell me whether it is your will that we go to Iceland.'

As he said that, a raven flew over his head. Ingolf watched it.

'It is Odin's will that we go,' he said. 'He sent his raven to tell us. It is flying straight toward Iceland.'

The men shouted with joy at that.

Now they hung some of the meat of the horses on a tree near the temple.

'For the ravens of Odin,' they said.

Ingolf carried the bowl of blood into the temple. He went through the feast hall in front to a little room at the back. Here stood wooden statues of the gods in a semicircle. Before them was a stone altar. Ingolf took a little brush of twigs that lay on it and dipped it into the blood and sprinkled the statues.

'You shall taste of our sacrifice,' he said. 'Look kindly on us from your happy seats in Asgard.'

Then they went into the feast hall. There thralls were boiling the horseflesh in pots over the fire. The tables were standing ready before the benches. Ingolf walked to the high seat. All the others took their places at the benches. When the horns came round, Ingolf made this vow:

'I vow that I will build my house wherever these pillars lead me.'

He put his hand upon a tall post that stood beside the high seat. There was one at each side. They were the front posts of the chair. But they stood up high, almost to the roof. They were wonderfully carved and painted with men and dragons. On the top of each one was a little statue of Thor with his hammer.

At the end of the feast Ingolf had his thralls dig these pillars up. He had a little bronze chest filled with the earth that was under the altar.

'I will take the pillars of my high seat to Iceland,' he said, 'and I will set up my altar there upon the soil of Norway, the soil that all my ancestors have trod, the soil that Thor loves.'

So they carried the pillars and the chest of earth and the statues of the gods, and put them into Ingolf's boat.

'It is a well-packed ship,' the men said. 'There is no spot to spare.'

Tools, and chests of food, and tubs of drink, and chests of clothes, and fishing nets were stowed in the bows of both boats. In the bottom were laid some long, heavy, hewn logs.

'The trees in Iceland are little,' Ingolf said. 'We must take the great beams for our homes with us.'

Standing on these logs were a few cattle and sheep and horses and pigs. The rowers' benches were along the sides. In the stern of each boat was a little cabin. Here the women and children were to sleep. But the men would sleep on the timbers in the middle of the boat and perhaps they would put up the awning sometimes.

At last everyone was aboard. Men loosed the rope that held the boats. The ships flashed down the rollers into the water, and Ingolf and Leif were off for Iceland. As they sailed away everyone looked back at the shore of old Norway. There were tears in the women's eyes. Helga, Leif's wife, sang:

> 'There was I born. There was I wed.
> There are my father's bones.
> There are the hills and fields,
> The streams and rocks that I love.
> There are houses and temples,

Women and warriors and feasts,
Ships and songs and fights –
A crowded, joyous land.
I go to an empty land.'

There was the same long voyage with storm and fog. But at last the people saw again the white cloud and saw it growing into land and mountains. Then Ingolf took the pillars of his high seat and threw them overboard.

'Guide them to a good place, O Thor!' he cried.

The waves caught them up and rolled them about. Ingolf followed them with his ship. But soon a storm came up. The men had to take down the sails and masts, and they could do nothing with their oars. The two ships tossed about in the sea wherever the waves sent them. The pillars drifted away, and Ingolf could not see them.

'Remember your pillars, O Thor!' he cried.

Then he saw that Leif's ship was being driven far off.

'Ah, my foster-brother,' he thought, 'shall I not have you to cheer me in this empty land? O Thor, let him not go down to the caves of Rán! He is too good a man for that.'

On the next day the storm was not so hard, and Ingolf put in at a good harbour. A high rocky point stuck out into the sea. A broad bay with islands in the mouth was at the side. Behind the rocky point was a level green place with ice-mountains shining far back.

After a day or two Ingolf said:

'I will go look for my pillars.'

So he and a few men got into the rowboat and went along the

'Then he saw that Leif's ship was being driven afar off'

shore and into all the fjords, but they could not find the pillars. After a week they came back, and Ingolf said:

'I will build a house here to live in while I look for the posts. This way is uncomfortable for the women.'

So he did. Then he set out again to look for the pillars, but he had no better luck and came back.

'I must stay at home and see to the making of hay and the drying of fish,' he said. 'Winter is coming on, and we must not be caught with nothing to eat.'

So he stayed and worked and sent two of his thralls to look for the holy posts. They came back every week or two and always had to say that they had not found them. Midwinter was coming on.

'Ah!' said Ingolf's wife one day, 'do you remember the gay feast that we had at Yule-time? All our friends were there. The house rang with song and laughter. Our tables bent with good things to eat. Walls were hung with gay draperies. The floor was clean with sweet-smelling pine-branches. Now look at this mean house; its dirt floor, its bare stone walls, its littleness, its darkness! Look at our long faces. No one here could make a song if he tried. Oh! I am sick for dear old Norway.'

'It is Thor's fault,' Ingolf cried. 'He will not let me find his posts.'

He strode out of the house and stood scowling at the grey sea.

'Ah, foster-brother!' he said. 'It was never so gloomy when you were by my side. Where are you now? Shall I never hear your merry laugh again? That spot in my palm burns, and my heart aches to see you. That arch of sod keeps rising before my eyes. Our vows keep ringing in my ears.'

At last the long, gloomy winter passed and spring came.

'Cheer up, good wife,' Ingolf said. 'Better days are coming now.'

But that same day the thralls came back from looking for the posts.

'We have bad news,' they said. 'As we walked along the shore looking for the pillars we saw a man lying on the shore. We went up to him. He was dead. It was Leif. Two well-built houses stood near. We went to them. We knew from the carving on the door-posts that they were Leif's. We went in. The rooms were empty. Along the shore and in the wood back of the house we found all of his men, dead. There was no living thing about.'

Ingolf said no word, but his face was white, and his mouth was set. He went into the house and got his spears and his shield and said to his men:

'Follow me.'

They put provisions into the boat and pushed off and sailed until they saw Leif's houses on the shore of the harbour. There they saw Leif and the men who were his friends, dead. Their swords and spears were gone. Ingolf walked through the houses calling on Helga and on the thralls, but no one answered. The storehouse was empty. The rich hangings were gone from the walls of the houses. There was nothing in the stables. The boat was gone.

Ingolf went out and stood on a high point of land that jutted out into the water. Far along the coast he saw some little islands. He turned to his men and said:

'The thralls have done it. I think we shall find them on those islands.'

Then he went back to Leif and stood looking at him.

'What a shame for so brave a man to fall by the hands of thralls! But I have found that such things always happen to men who do not sacrifice to the gods. Ah, Leif! I did not think when we made those vows of foster-brotherhood that this would ever happen. But do not fear. I remember my promise. I had thought that a man's blood is precious in this empty land, but my vow is more precious.'

Now they laid all those men together and tied on their hell-shoes.

'I need my sword for your sake, foster-brother. I cannot give you that. But you shall have my spears and my drinking-horn,' said Ingolf. 'For surely Odin has chosen you for Valhalla, even though you did not sacrifice. You are too good a man to go to Niflheim. You would make times merry in Valhalla.'

So Ingolf put his spears and his drinking-horn by Leif. Then the men raised a great mound over all the dead. After that they went aboard their boat and sailed for the islands that Ingolf had seen. It was evening when they reached them.

'I see smoke rising from that one,' Ingolf said, pointing.

He steered for it. It was a steep rock like that one in the Faroes, but they found a harbour and landed and climbed the steep hill and came out on top. They saw the ten thralls sitting about a bonfire eating. Helga and the other women from Leif's house sat near, huddled together, white and frightened. One of the thralls gave a great laugh and shouted:

'This is better than pulling Leif's plough. Tomorrow we will sail for Ireland with all his wealth.'

'Tomorrow you will be freezing in Niflheim,' cried Ingolf, and he leaped among them swinging his sword, and all his men followed him, and they killed those thralls.

Then Ingolf turned to Helga. She threw herself into his arms and wept. But after a while she told him this story:

'When springtime came, Leif thought that he would sow wheat. He had but one ox. The others had died during the winter. So he set the thralls to help pull the plough. I saw their sour looks and was afraid, but Leif only laughed:

'"What else can thralls expect?" he said. "Never fear them, good wife."

'Now one day soon after that the thralls came running to the house calling out:

'"The ox is dead! The ox is dead!"

'Leif asked them about it. They said that a bear had come out of the woods and killed it, and that they had scared the beast away. They pointed out where it had gone. Then Leif called his men and said:

'"A hunt! I had not hoped for such great sport here. Ah, we will have a feast off that bear!"

'So they took their spears and went out into the woods. As soon as they were gone, the thralls came running into the house and took down all the swords and shields from the wall and ran out. In some way they met my lord and his men in the woods and killed them. Then they came back and took everything in the house and dragged us to the boat and sailed here.'

'O my brother!' said Ingolf, 'where is that song about "those two foster-brothers, Ingolf and Leif, who made a new country in a wonderful land, and whose sons and grandsons are mighty men in Iceland"? But come home with me, Helga.'

So they took the women and Leif's things and Leif's boat and sailed home. The next day after they came to Ingolf's house, Helga said:

'We have made your family larger, brother Ingolf. Will you not take Leif's two houses and live in them? He does not need them now. He would like you to have them.'

'It would be pleasant to live there,' Ingolf said. 'I thank you.'

So the next day they loaded everything aboard the two ships and sailed for Leif's house. There they stayed for a year. Ingolf still sent his thralls out to look for the pillars. He was careful always to have hay, so his cattle prospered. That spring he planted wheat, but it did not grow well.

'This is sickly stuff,' Ingolf said. 'It takes too much time and work. It is better to save the land for hay. Perhaps we can sometime go back to Norway for flour.'

At last one day the thralls came home and said:

'We have found the pillars.'

Ingolf jumped to his feet. He cried out:

'You have kept me waiting three years, Thor. But as soon as my house and temple are built, I will sacrifice to you three horses as a thank-offering.'

'It is a long way off, master,' the thralls said, 'and we have found much better places in our walks about the island.'

'Thor knows best,' Ingolf answered. 'I will settle where he leads me.'

So that summer they loaded everything into the ships again

and sailed west along the coast until they came to the place where the pillars were. The land there was low and green. On both sides were low hills. A little lake glistened back from shore. In the valley were hot springs, with steam rising from them.

'It looks like smoke,' the men said. 'It is very strange to see hot water and smoke come out of the ground.'

In front of this green land was a good harbour with islands in it. Far over the sea toward the north shone a great ice-mountain.

'I like the place,' Ingolf said. 'I will make this land mine.'

So he built fires at the mouth of the river near there, and stood by them and called out loudly:

'I have put my fire at the mouth of these rivers. All the land that they drain is mine, and no man shall claim it but me. I will call this place Reykjavik.'

Then Ingolf built his feast hall. He himself carved the beams and the door-posts. Gaily painted dragons leaned out from the doors and stood up from the gables. Men and animals fought on the door-posts. For the doors he made at the forge great iron hinges. Their ends curved and spread all over the door. Near his feast hall he built a storehouse and a kitchen and a smithy and a stable and a bower for the women.

'We do not need a sleeping-house for guests,' he said. 'Who would be our guests?'

He roofed all his buildings with turf. It made them look like green mounds with gay carved and painted walls under them. He built also a temple, and on that was beautiful carving. In this he set up those statues that had been in his old temple. He put up, too, those pillars of his high seat that had been drifting about so long. Under them he laid the soil of Norway that he had brought in the little bronze chest.

'I have kept my vow, O Thor!' he cried.

Then he sacrificed three horses that he had promised to Thor. After that was over, he said:

'Here is a good field for sport. Let us have some of the old games that we used to play at home. Who will wrestle with me?'

So they wrestled there and ran races and swam in the water. The women sat and looked on.

'Oh, this is good to see!' Helga cried. 'We are as gay as we used to be in old Norway.'

But it was not many weeks before Ingolf said:

'I wish that I might sometime see sails in that harbour. I wish that I might think, "Around this point of land is another farm, and across the bay is another. I can go there when I am very lonely." I wish that I might sometime be invited to a feast. I wish that I might sometimes hear the good, clanging music of weapons at play. It is a good land, but we have lived alone for four years. I am hungry for new faces and for tidings of Norway.'

One night as he and his men sat about the long fire in the feast hall, a servant threw a great piece of wood upon the fire. It was streaked with faded paint and it showed bits of carving.

'See,' said Ingolf, pointing to it, 'see what is left of a good ship's prow! What lands have you seen, O dragon's head? What battles have you fought? What was your master's name? Where did the storm meet you? Perhaps he was coming to Iceland, comrades. Would it not have been pleasant to see his sail and to shake his hand and to welcome him to Iceland? But instead he is in Rán's caves, and only his broken prow has drifted here.'

Now it was not many months after that when one of the men came running into the feast hall, shouting:

'A sail! a sail in the harbour!'

All those men gave a shout with no word in it, as though their hearts had leaped into their throats. They jumped up and ran to the shore and stood there with hungry eyes. When the men landed, those Icelanders clapped them on the shoulders, and tears ran down their faces. For a long time they could say nothing but 'Welcome! Welcome!'

But after a while Ingolf led them to the feast hall and had a feast spread at once. While the thralls were at work, the men stood together and talked. Such a noise had never been in that hall before.

'We have already built our fires and claimed our land up the shore a way,' the leader said. 'Men in Norway talk much of Ingolf and Leif, and wonder what has happened to them.'

Then Ingolf told them of all that had come to pass in Iceland; and then he asked of Norway.

'Ah! things are going from bad to worse,' the newcomers said. 'Harald grows mightier every day. A man dare not swing a sword now except for the king. We came here to get away from him. Many men are talking of Iceland. Soon the sea-road between here and Norway will be swarming with dragons.'

And so it was. Ships also came from Ireland and from the Shetlands and the Orkneys.

'Harald has come west-over-seas,' the men of these ships said, 'and has laid his heavy hand upon the islands and put his jarls over

'Those Icelanders clapped them on the shoulders'

them. They are no place now for free men.'

So by the time Ingolf was an old man, Iceland was no longer an empty land. Every valley was spotted with bright feast halls and temples. Horses and cattle pastured on the hillsides. Smoke curled up from kitchens and smithies. Gay ships sailed the waters, taking Iceland cloth and wool and Iceland fish and oil and the soft feathers of Iceland birds to Norway to sell, and bringing back wood and flour and grain.

When Ingolf died, his men drew up on the shore the boat in which he had come to Iceland. They painted it freshly and put new gold on it, so that it stood there a glittering dragon with head raised high, looking over the water. Old Sighvat lifted a huge stone and carried it to the ship's side. With all his strength he threw it into the bottom. The timbers cracked.

'If this ship moves from here,' he said, 'then I do not know how to moor a ship. It is Ingolf's grave.'

Then men laid Ingolf upon his shield and carried him and placed him on the high deck in the stern near the pilot's seat where he had sat to steer to Iceland. They hung his sword over his shoulder. They laid his spear by his side. In his hand they put his mead-horn. Into the ship they set a great treasure-chest filled with beautiful clothes and bracelets and head-bands. Beside the treasure-chest they piled up many swords and spears and shields. They put gold-trimmed saddles and bridles upon three horses. Then they killed the horses and dragged them into the ship. They killed hunting-dogs and put them by the horses; for they said:

'All these things Ingolf will need in Valhalla. When he walks through the door of that feast hall, Odin must know that a rich and brave man comes. When he fights with those heroes during the day, he must have weapons worthy of him. He must have dogs for the hunt. When he feasts with those heroes at night he must wear rich clothes, so that those feasters shall know that he was a wealthy man and generous, and that his friends loved him.'

Ingolf's son tied on his hell-shoes for the long journey.

'If these shoes come untied,' he said, 'I do not know how to fasten hell-shoes.'

Then he went out of the ship and stood on the ground with his family.

All the men of Iceland were there.

'This is a glorious sight,' they said. 'Surely no ship ever carried a richer load. Inside and out the boat blazes with gold and bronze, and, high over his riches, lies the great Ingolf, ready to take the tiller and guide to Valhalla, where all the heroes will rise up and shout him welcome.'

Then the thralls heaped a mound of earth over the ship. This hill stood up against the sky and seemed to say: 'Here lies a great man.' Sighvat put a stone on the top, with runes on it telling whose grave it was. All this time a skald stood by and played on his harp and sang a song about that time when Ingolf came to Iceland. He called him the father of Iceland. People of that country still read an old story that the men of that long ago time wrote about Ingolf, and they love him because he was a brave man and 'the first of men to come to Iceland'.

Eric the Red

It was a spring day many years after Ingolf died. All the freemen in the west of Iceland had come to a meeting. Here they made laws and punished men for having done wrong. The meeting was over now. Men were walking about the plain and talking. Everybody seemed much excited. Voices were loud, arms were swinging.

'It was an unjust decision,' some one cried. 'Eric killed the men in fair fight. The judges outlawed him because they were afraid. His foe Thorgest has many rich and powerful men to back him.'

'No, no!' said another. 'Eric is a bloody man. I am glad he is out of Iceland.'

Just then a big man with bushy red hair and beard stalked through the crowd. He looked straight ahead and scowled.

'There he goes,' people said, and turned to look after him.

'His hands are as red as his beard,' some said, and frowned.

But others looked at him and smiled, saying:

'He walks like Thor the Fearless.'

'His story would make a fine song,' one said. 'As strong and as brave and as red as Thor! Always in a quarrel. A man of many

‘He looked straight ahead of him and scowled’

places – Norway, the north of Iceland, the west of Iceland, those little islands off the shore of Iceland. Outlawed from all of them on account of his quarrels. Where will he go now, I wonder?'

This Eric strode down to the shore with his men following.

'He is in a black temper,' they said. 'We should best not talk to him.'

So they made ready the boat in silence. Eric got into the pilot's seat and they sailed off. Soon they pulled the ship up on their own shore. Eric strolled into his house and called for supper. When the drinking-horns had been filled and emptied, Eric pulled himself up and smiled and shouted out so that the great room was full of his big voice:

'There is no friend like mead. It always cheers a man's heart.'

Then laughter and talking began in the hall because Eric's good temper had come back. After a while Eric said:

'Well, I must off somewhere. I have been driven about from place to place, like a seabird in a storm. And there is always a storm about me. It is my sword's fault. She is ever itching to break her peace-bands and be out and at the play. She has shut Norway to me and now Iceland. Where will you go next, old comrade?' and he pulled out his sword and looked at it and smiled as the fire flashed on it.

'There are some of us who will follow you wherever you go, Eric,' called a man from across the fire.

'Is it so?' Eric cried, leaping up. 'Oh! then we shall have some merry times yet. Who will go with me?'

More than half the men in the hall jumped to their feet and waved their drinking-horns and shouted:

'More than half the men in the hall jumped to their feet'

'I! I!'

Eric sat down in his chair and laughed.

'O you bloody birds of battle!' he cried. 'Ever hungry for new frolic! Our swords are sisters in blood, and we are brothers in adventure. Do you know what is in my heart to do?'

He jumped to his feet, and his face glowed. Then he laughed as he looked at his men.

'I see the answer flashing from your eyes,' he said, 'that you will do it even if it is to go down to Niflheim and drag up Hela, the pale queen of the stiff dead.'

His men pounded on the tables and shouted:

'Yes! Yes! Anywhere behind Eric!'

'But it is not to Niflheim,' Eric laughed. 'Did you ever hear that story that Gunnbiorn told? He was sailing for Iceland, but the fog came down, and then the wind caught him and blew him far off. While he drifted about he saw a strange land that rose up white and shining out of a blue sea. Huge ships of ice sailed out from it and met him. I mean to sail to that land.'

A great shout went up that shook the rafters. Then the men sat and talked over plans. While they sat, a stranger came into the hall.

'I have no time to drink,' he said. 'I have a message from your friend Eyjolf. He says that Thorgest with all his men means to come here and catch you tonight. Eyjolf bids you come to him, and he will hide you until you are ready to start; for he loves you.'

'Hunted like a wolf from corner to corner of the world!' Eric cried angrily. 'Will they not even let me finish one feast?'

Then he laughed.

'But if I take my sport like a wolf, I must be hunted like one. So we shall sleep tonight in the woods about Eyjolf's house, comrades, instead of in these good beds. Well, we have done it before.'

'And it is no bad place,' cried some of the men.

'I always liked the stars better than a smoky house fire,' said one.

'Can no bad fortune spoil your good nature?' laughed Eric. 'But now we are off. Let every man carry what he can.'

So they quickly loaded themselves with clothes and gold and swords and spears and kettles of food. Eric led his wife Thorhild and his two young sons, Thorstein and Leif. All together they got into the boat and went to Eyjolf's farm. For a week or more they stayed in his woods, sometimes in a secret cave of his when they knew that Thorgest was about. And sometimes Eyjolf sent and said:

'Thorgest is off. Come to my house for a feast.'

All this time they were making ready for the voyage, repairing the ship and filling it with stores. Word of what Eric meant to do got out, and men laughed and said:

'Is that not like Eric? What will he not do?'

Some men liked the sound of it, and they came to Eric and said:

'We will go with you to this strange land.'

So all were ready and they pushed off with Eric's family aboard and those friends who had joined him. They took horses and cattle with them, and all kinds of tools and food.

'I do not well know where this land is,' Eric said. 'Gunnbiorn said only that he sailed east when he came home to Iceland. So I will steer straight west. We shall surely find something. I do not know, either, how long we must go.'

So they sailed that strange ocean, never dreaming what might be ahead of them. They found no islands to rest on. They met heavy fogs.

One day as Eric sat in the pilot's seat, he said:

'I think that I see one of Gunnbiorn's ships of ice. Shall we sail up to her and see what kind of a craft she is?'

'Yes,' shouted his men.

So they went on toward it.

'It sends out a cold breath,' said one of the men.

They all wrapped their cloaks about them.

'It is a bigger boat than I ever saw before,' said Eric. 'The white mast stands as high as a hill.'

'It must be giants that sail in it, frost giants,' said another of the men.

But as they came nearer, Eric all at once laughed loudly and called out:

'By Thor, that Gunnbiorn was a foolish fellow. Why, look! It is only a piece of floating ice such as we sometimes see from Iceland. It is no ship, and there is no one on it.'

His men laughed and one called to another and said:

'And you thought of frost giants!'

Then they sailed on for days and days. They met many of these icebergs.

On one of them was a white bear.

'Yonder is a strange pilot,' Eric laughed.

'I have seen bears come floating so to the north shore of Iceland,' an old man said. 'Perhaps they come from the land that we are going to find.'

"It is a bigger boat than I ever saw before"

One day Eric said:

'I see afar off an iceberg larger than any one yet. Perhaps that is our white land.'

But even as he said it he felt his boat swing under his hand as he held the tiller. He bore hard on the rudder, but he could not turn the ship.

'What is this?' he cried. 'A strong river is running here. It is carrying our ship away from this land. I cannot make head against it. Out with the oars!'

So with oars and sail and rudder they fought against the current, but it took the boat along like a chip, and after a while they put up their oars and drifted.

'Luck has taken us into its own hands,' Eric laughed. 'But this is as good a way as another.'

Sometimes they were near enough to see the land, then they were carried out into the sea and thought that they should never see any land again.

'Perhaps this river will carry us to a whirlpool and suck us under,' the men said.

But at last Eric felt the current less strong under his hand.

'To the oars again!' he called.

So they fought with the current and sailed out of it and went on toward land. But when they reached the shore they found no place to go in. Steep black walls shot up from the sea. Nothing grew on them. When the men looked above the cliffs they saw a long line of white cutting the sky.

'It is a land of ice,' they said.

They sailed on south, all the time looking for a place to go ashore.

'I am sick of this endless sea,' Thorhild complained, 'but this land is worse.'

After a while they began to see small bays cut into the shore with little flat patches of green at their sides. They landed in these places and stretched and warmed themselves and ate.

'But these spots are only big enough for graves,' the men said. 'We cannot live here.'

So they went on again. All the time the weather was growing colder. Eric's people kept themselves wrapped in their cloaks and put scarfs around their heads.

'And it is still summer!' Thorhild said. 'What will it be in winter?'

'We must find a place to build a house now before the winter comes on,' said Eric. 'We must not freeze here.'

So they chose a little spot with hills about it to keep off the wind. They made a house out of stones; for there were many in that place. They lived there that winter. The sea for a long way out from shore froze so that it looked like white land. The men went out upon it to hunt white bear and seal. They ate the meat and wore the skins to keep them warm. The hardest thing was to get fuel for the fire. No trees grew there. The men found a little driftwood along the shore, but it was not enough. So they burned the bones and the fat of the animals they killed.

'It is a sickening smell,' Thorhild said. 'I have not been out of this mean house for weeks. I am tired of the darkness and the smoke and the cattle. And all the time I hear great noises, as though some giant were breaking this land into pieces.'

'Ah, cheer up, good wife!' Eric laughed. 'I smell better luck ahead.'

Once Eric and his men climbed the cliffs and went back into the middle of the land. When they came home they had this to tell:

'It is a country of ice, shining white. Nothing grows on it but a few mosses. Far off it looks flat, but when you walk upon it, there are great holes and cracks. We could see nothing beyond. There seems to be only a fringe of land around the edge of an island of ice.'

The winter nights were very long. Sometimes the sun showed for an hour, sometimes for only a few minutes, sometimes it did not show at all for a week. The men hunted by the bright shining of the moon or by the northern lights.

As it grew warmer the ice in the sea began to crack and move and melt and float away. Eric waited only until there was a clear passage in the water. Then he launched his boat, and they sailed southward again. At last they found a place that Eric liked.

'Here I will build my house,' he said.

So they did and lived there that summer and pastured their cattle and cut hay for the winter and fished and hunted.

The next spring Eric said:

'The land stretches far north. I am hungry to know what is there.'

Then they all got into the boat again and sailed north.

'We can leave no one here,' Eric had said. 'We cannot tell what might come between us. Perhaps giants or dragons or strange men might come out of this inland ice and kill our people. We must stay together.'

Farther north they found only the same bare, frozen country. So after a while they sailed back to their home and lived there.

One spring after they had been in that land for four years, Eric said:

'My eyes are hungry for the sight of men and green fields again. My stomach is sick of seal and whale and bear. My throat is dry for mead. This is a bare and cold and hungry land. I will visit my friends in Iceland.'

'And our swords are rusty with long resting,' said his men. 'Perhaps we can find play for them in Iceland.'

'Now I have a plan,' Eric suddenly said. 'Would it not be pleasant to see other feast halls as we sail along the coast?'

'Oh! it would be a beautiful sight,' his men said.

'Well,' said Eric, 'I am going to try to bring back some neighbours from Iceland. Now we must have a name for our land. How does Greenland sound?'

His men laughed and said:

'It is a very white Greenland, but men will like the sound of it. It is better than Iceland.'

So Eric and all his people sailed back and spent the winter with his friends.

'Ah! Eric, it is good to hear your laugh again,' they said.

Eric was at many feasts and saw many men, and he talked much of his Greenland.

'The sea is full of whale and seals and great fish,' he said. 'The land has bear and reindeer. There are no men there. Come back with me and choose your land.'

Many men said that they would do it. Some men went because they thought it would be a great frolic to go to a new country. Some went because they were poor in Iceland and thought:

'I can be no worse off in Greenland, and perhaps I shall grow rich there.'

And some went because they loved Eric and wanted to be his neighbours.

So the next summer thirty-five ships full of men and women and goods followed Eric for Greenland. But they met heavy storms, and some ships were wrecked, and the men drowned. Other men grew heartsick at the terrible storm and the long voyage and no sight of land, and they turned back to Iceland. So of those thirty-five ships only fifteen got to Greenland.

'Only the bravest and the luckiest men come here,' Eric said. 'We shall have good neighbours.'

Soon other houses were built along the fjords.

'It is pleasant to sail along the coast now,' said Eric. 'I see smoke rising from houses and ships standing on the shore and friendly hands waving.'

Leif and His New Land

Now Eric had lived in Greenland for fifteen years. His sons Thorstein and Leif had grown up to be big, strong men. One spring Leif said to his father:

'I have never seen Norway, our mother land. I long to go there and meet the great men and see the places that skalds sing about.'

Eric answered:

'It is right that you should go. No man has really lived until he has seen Norway.'

So he helped Leif fit out a boat and sent him off. Leif sailed for months. He passed Iceland and the Faroes and the Shetlands. He stopped at all of these places and feasted his mind on the new things. And everywhere men received him gladly; for he was handsome and wise. But at last he came near Norway. Then he stood up before the pilot's seat and sang loudly:

'My eyes can see her at last,
The mother of mighty men,
The field of famous fights.
In the sky above I see

Fair Asgard's shining roofs,
The flying hair of Thor,
The wings of Odin's birds,
The road that heroes tread.
I am here in the land of the gods,
The land of mighty men.'

For a while he walked the land as though he were in a dream. He looked at this and that and everything and loved them all because it was Norway.

'I will go to the king,' he said.

He had never seen a king. There were no kings in Iceland or in Greenland. So he went to the city where the king had his fine house. The king's name was Olaf. He was a great-grandson of Harald Hairfair; for Harald had been dead a hundred years.

Now the king was going to hold a feast at night, and Leif put on his most beautiful clothes to go to it. He put on long tights of blue wool and a short jacket of blue velvet. He belted his jacket with a gold girdle. He had shoes of scarlet with golden clasps. He threw around himself a cape of scarlet velvet lined with seal fur. His long sword stuck out from under his cloak. On his head he put a knitted cap of bright colours. Then he walked to the king's feast hall and went through the door. It was a great hall, and it was full of richly-dressed men. The fires shone on so many golden headbands and bracelets and so many glittering swords and spears on the wall, and there was so much noise of talking and laughing, that at first Leif did not know what to do. But at last he went and sat on the very end seat of the bench near him.

As the feast went on, King Olaf sat in his high seat and looked about the hall and noticed this one and that one and spoke across the fire to many. He was keen-eyed and soon saw Leif in his far seat.

'Yonder is some man of mark,' he said to himself. 'He is surely worth knowing. His face is not the face of a fool. He carries his head like a lord of men.'

He sent a thrall and asked Leif to come to him. So Leif walked down the long hall and stood before the king.

'I am glad to have you for a guest,' the king said. 'What are your name and country?'

'I am Leif Ericsson, and I have come all the way from Greenland to see you and old Norway.'

'From Greenland!' said the king. 'It is not often that I see a Greenlander. Many come to Norway to trade, but they seldom come to the king's hall. I shall be glad to hear about your land. Come up and speak with me.'

So Leif went up the steps of the high seat and sat down by the king and talked with him. When the feast was over the king said:

'You shall live at my court this winter, Leif Ericsson. You are a welcome guest.'

So Leif stayed there that winter. When he started back in the spring, the king gave him two thralls as a parting gift.

'Let this gift show my love, Leif Ericsson,' he said. 'For your sake I shall not forget Greenland.'

Leif sailed back again and had good luck until he was past Iceland. Then great winds came out of the north and tossed his ship about so that the men could do nothing. They were blown south for days and days. They did not know where they were. Then they saw land, and Leif said:

'Surely luck has brought us also to a new country. We will go in and see what kind of a place it is.'

So he steered for it. As they came near, the men said:

'See the great trees and the soft, green shore. Surely this is a better country than Greenland or than Iceland either.'

When they landed they threw themselves upon the ground.

'I never lay on a bed so soft as this grass,' one said.

'Taller trees do not grow in Norway,' said another.

'There is no stone here as in Norway, but only good black dirt,' Leif said. 'I never saw so fertile a land before.'

The men were hungry and set about building a fire.

'There is no lack of fuel here,' they said.

They stayed many days in this country and walked about to see what was there. A German, named Tyrker, was with Leif. He was a little man with a high forehead and a short nose. His eyes were big and rolling. He had lived with Eric for many years, and had taken care of Leif when he was a little boy. So Leif loved him.

Now one day they had been wandering about and all came back to camp at night except Tyrker. When Leif looked around on his comrades, he said:

'Where is Tyrker?'

No one knew. Then Leif was angry.

'Is a man of so little value in this empty land that you would lose one?' he said. 'Why did you not keep together? Did you not see that he was gone? Why did you not set out to look for him? Who knows what terrible thing may have happened to him in

these great forests?'

Then he turned and started out to hunt for him. His men followed, silent and ashamed. They had not gone far when they saw Tyrker running toward them. He was laughing and talking to himself. Leif ran to him and put his arms about him with gladness at seeing him.

'Why are you so late?' he asked. 'Where have you been?'

But Tyrker, still smiling and nodding his head, answered in German. He pointed to the woods and laughed and rolled his eyes. Again Leif asked his question and put his hand on Tyrker's shoulder as though he would shake him. Then Tyrker answered in the language of Iceland:

'I have not been so very far, but I have found something wonderful.'

'What is it?' cried the men.

'I have found grapes growing wild,' answered Tyrker, and he laughed, and his eyes shone.

'It cannot be,' Leif said.

Grapes do not grow in Greenland nor in Iceland nor even in Norway. So it seemed a wonderful thing to these Norsemen.

'Can I not tell grapes when I see them?' cried Tyrker. 'Did I not grow up in Germany, where every hillside is covered with grapevines? Ah! it seems like my old home.'

'It is wonderful,' Leif said. 'I have heard travellers tell of seeing grapes growing, but I myself never saw it. You shall take us to them early in the morning, Tyrker.'

So in the morning they went back into the woods and saw the grapes. They ate of them.

'He pointed to the woods and laughed and rolled his eyes'

'They are like food and drink,' they cried.

That day Leif said:

'We spent most of the summer on the ocean. Winter will soon be coming on and the sea about Greenland will be frozen. We must start back. I mean to take some of the things of this land to show to our people at home. We will fill the rowboat with grapes and tow it behind us. The ship we will load with logs from these great trees. That will be a welcome shipload in Greenland, where we have neither trees nor vines. Now half of you shall gather grapes for the next few days, and the other half shall cut timber.'

So they did, and after a week sailed off. The ship was full of lumber, and they towed the rowboat loaded with grapes. As they looked back at the shore, Leif said:

'I will call this country Wineland for the grapes that grow there.'

One of the men leaped upon the gunwale and leaned out, clinging to the sail, and sang:

'Wineland the good, Wineland the warm,
Wineland the green, the great, the fat.
Our dragon fed and crawls away
With belly stuffed and lazy feet.
How long her purple, trailing tail!
She fed and grew to twice her size.'

Then all the men waved their hands to the shore and gave a great shout for that good land.

For all that voyage they had fair weather and sailed into Eric's harbour before the winter came. Eric saw the ship and ran down to the shore. He took Leif into his arms and said:

'Oh, my son, my old eyes ached to see you. I hunger to hear of all that you have seen and done.'

'Luck has followed me all the way,' said Leif. 'See what I have brought home.'

The Greenlanders looked.

'Lumber! lumber!' they cried. 'Oh! it is better stuff than gold.'

Then they saw the grapes and tasted them.

'Surely you must have plundered Asgard,' they said, smacking their lips.

At the feast that night Eric said:

'Leif shall sit in the place of honour.'

So Leif sat in the high seat opposite Eric. All men thought him a handsome and wise man. He told them of the storm and of Wineland.

'No man would ever need a cloak there. The soil is richer than the soil of Norway. Grain grows wild, and you yourselves saw the grapes that we got from there. The forests are without end. The sea is full of fish.'

The Greenlanders listened with open mouths to all this. They turned and talked to Leif's ship-comrades who were scattered among them.

Leif noticed two strangers, an old man who sat at Eric's side and a young woman on the cross-bench. He turned to his brother Thorstein who sat next to him.

'Who are these strangers?' he asked.

'Thorbiorn and his daughter Gudrid,' Thorstein answered.

'They landed here this spring. I never saw our father more glad of anything than to see this Thorbiorn. They were friends before we left Iceland. When they saw each other again they could not talk enough of old times. In the spring Eric means to give him a farm up the fjord a way. It seems that this Thorbiorn comes of a good family that has been rich and great in Iceland for years. And Thorbiorn himself was rich when our father knew him, and was much honoured by all men. But ill luck came, and he grew poor. This hurt his pride. "I will not stay in Iceland and be a beggar," he said to himself. "I will not have men look at me and say, 'He is not what his father was.' I will go to my friend Eric the Red in Greenland."

'Then he got ready a great feast and invited all his friends. It was such a feast as had not been in Iceland for years. Thorbiorn spent on it all the wealth that he had left. For he said to himself, "I will not leave in shame. Men shall remember my last feast." After that he set out and came to Greenland.

'Is not Gudrid beautiful? And she is wise. I mean to marry her, if her father will permit it.'

Now Leif settled down in Greenland and became a great man there. He was so busy and he grew so rich that he did not think of going to Wineland again. But people could not forget his story. Many nights as men sat about the long fires they talked of that wonderful land and wished to see it.

Wineland the Good

On an autumn, a year or two after Leif came home, Eric and his men saw two large ships come to land not far down the shore from the house.

'They look like trading ships,' Eric said. 'Let us go down to see them.'

'I will go, too,' Gudrid said. 'Perhaps they will have rich cloth and jewellry. It is long since I had my eyes on a new dress.'

So they all went down and found two large trading ships lying in the water. A great many men were on the shore making a fire.

'Welcome to Greenland!' called Eric. 'What are your names and your country?'

Then a fine, big man walked out from among the men and went up to Eric.

'I am Thorfinn,' he said, 'a trader. I sailed this summer from Iceland with forty men and a shipload of goods. On the sea I met this other ship from Iceland. The master is Biarni. Come and look at my goods.'

So he rowed Eric and Gudrid out and they went aboard his boat. Thorfinn opened his chests and showed Eric gleaming swords and bracelets and axes and farm tools. But before Gudrid he spread beautiful cloth and gold embroidery and golden necklaces. As they looked, he told of doings in Iceland and asked of Greenland.

'We never see such things as these in this bare land,' Gudrid said, as she smoothed a beautiful dress of purple velvet. 'I envy the women of Iceland their fair clothes.'

'There is no need of that,' Thorfinn said, 'for this dress is yours and anything else from my chests that you like. Here is a necklace that I beg you to take. It did not have a fairer mistress in Greece where I got it.'

'You are a very generous trader,' Gudrid said.

Then Thorfinn gave Eric a great sword with a gold-studded scabbard. After a while he took them to Biarni's ship. He also gave them gifts. They all talked and laughed much while they were together.

'You are merry comrades,' Eric said. 'I ask you both and all your men to spend the winter at my house. You can put your goods into my storehouses.'

'By my sword! a generous offer,' said Thorfinn. 'As for me, I am happy to come.'

Biarni and all the rest said the same thing. Thorfinn walked to the house with Eric and Gudrid, while the other men sailed to the ship-sheds and pulled their boats under them.

Then Thorfinn saw to the unloading and storing of his goods.

'Is this Gudrid your daughter?' he asked of Eric one day.

'She is the widow of my son Thorstein,' Eric said. 'He died the same winter that they were married. Her father, too, died not long ago. So Gudrid lives with me.'

Now all that winter until Yule-time Eric spread a good feast every night. There was laughter through his house all the time. Often at the feasts the men cast lots to see whether they might sit on the cross-bench with the women. Sometimes it was Thorfinn's luck to sit by Gudrid. Then they talked gaily and drank together.

At last Yule was coming near. Eric went about the house gloomy then. One day Thorfinn put his hand on Eric's shoulder and said:

'Something is troubling you, Eric. We have all noticed that you are not gay as you used to be. Tell me what is the matter.'

'You have carried yourselves like noble men in my house,' Eric answered. 'I am proud to have you for guests. Now I am ashamed that you should not find a house worthy of you. I am ashamed that when you leave me you will have to say that you never spent a worse Yule than you did with Eric the Red in Greenland. For my cupboards are empty.'

'Oh, that is easily mended,' Thorfinn said. 'No house could feed eighty men so long and not feel it. I never knew so generous a host before. But I have flour and grain and mead in my boat. You are welcome to all of it. You have only to open the doors of your own storehouses. It is a little gift.'

So Eric used those things, and there was never a merrier Yule feast than in his house that winter.

When Yule was over, Thorfinn said to Eric:

'Gudrid is a beautiful and wise woman. I wish to have her for my wife.'

'You seem to be a man worthy of her,' Eric said.

So that winter Gudrid and Thorfinn were married and lived at Eric's house.

One day Thorfinn said to Eric:

'I have heard much of this wonderful Wineland since I have been here. It seems to me that it is worth while to go and see more of it.'

'My son Thorstein and I tried it once,' said Eric. 'It was the year after Leif came back. We set out with a fair ship and with glad hearts, but we tossed about all summer on the sea and got nowhere. We were wet with storm, lean with hunger and illness, and heartsick at our bad luck.'

'And yet,' Thorfinn said, 'another time we might have better weather. I have never seen so fair a land as this seems to be.'

Then he went to Leif and talked long with him. Leif told him in what direction he had sailed to come home, and how the shores looked that he had passed.

'I think I could find my way,' Thorfinn said. 'My heart moves me to try this frolic.'

He spoke to Gudrid about it.

'Oh, yes!' she cried. 'Let us go. It is long since I felt a boat leaping under me. I am tired of sitting still. I want to feel the warm days and see the soft grass and the high trees and taste the grapes of this Wineland the Good.'

Then he talked with his men and with Biarni.

'We are ready,' they all said. 'We are only waiting for a leader.'

'Then let us go!' cried Thorfinn.

So in the spring they fitted up their two ships and put into them provisions and a few cattle. Some of Eric's men also got ready a boat, so that three ships set sail from Eric's harbour carrying one hundred and sixty men to Wineland. As they started, Gudrid stood on the deck and sang:

'I will feast my eyes on new things –
On mighty trees and purple grapes,
On beds of flowers and soft grass.
I will sun myself in a warm land.'

They sailed on and past those shores that Leif had spoken of. Whenever they saw any interesting place they sailed in and looked about and rested there.

They had gone far south, past many fair shores with woods on them, when Gudrid said one day:

'This is a beautiful bay with a smooth, green field by it, and the great mountains far back. I should like to stay there for a little while.'

So they sailed in and drew their ships up on shore. They put up the awnings in them.

'These shall be our houses,' Thorfinn said.

They were strange-looking houses – shining dragons with gay backs lying on the yellow sand. Near them the Norsemen lighted fires and cooked their supper. That night they slept in the ships. In the morning Gudrid said:

'I long to see what is back of that mountain.'

So they all climbed it. When they stood on the top they could see far over the country.

'There is a lake that we must see,' Thorfinn said.

'I should like to sail around that bay,' said Biarni, pointing.

'I am going to walk up that valley yonder,' one of the men said.

And everyone saw some place where he would like to go. So

for all that summer they camped in that spot and went about the country seeing new things. They hunted in the woods and caught rabbits and birds and sometimes bears and deer. Every day some men rowed out to sea and fished. There was an island in the bay where thousands of birds had their nests. The men gathered eggs here.

'We have more to eat than we had in Greenland or Iceland,' Thorfinn said, 'and need not work at all. It is all play.'

Near the end of summer Thorfinn spoke to his comrades.

'Have we not seen everything here? Let us go to a new place. We have not yet found grapes.'

Thorfinn and Biarni and all their men sailed south again. But some of Eric's men went off in their boat another way. Years afterward the Greenlanders heard that they were shipwrecked and made slaves in Ireland.

After Thorfinn and Biarni had sailed for many days they landed on a low, green place. There were hills around it. A little lake was there.

'What is growing on those hillsides?' Thorfinn said, shading his eyes with his hand.

He and some others ran up there. The people on shore heard them shout.

Soon they came running back with their hands full of something.

'Grapes! Grapes!' they were shouting.

All those people sat down and ate the grapes and then went to the hillside and picked more.

'Now we are indeed in Wineland,' they said. 'It is as wonderful as Leif's stories. Surely we must stay here for a long time.'

The very next day they went into the woods and began to cut out lumber. The huts that they built were little things. They had no windows, and in the doorways the men hung their cloaks instead of doors.

'We can be out in the air so much in this warm country,' said Gudrid, 'that we do not need fine houses.'

The huts were scattered all about, some on the side of the lake, some at the shore of the harbour, some on the hillside. Gudrid had said:

'I want to live by the lake where I can look into the green woods and hear sweet bird-noises.'

So Thorfinn built his hut there.

As they sat about the campfire one night, Biarni said:

'It is strange that so good a land should be empty. I suppose that these are the first houses that were ever built in Wineland. It is wonderful to think that we are alone here in this great land.'

All that winter no snow fell. The cattle pastured on the grass.

'To think of the cold, frozen winters in Greenland!' Gudrid said. 'Oh! this is the sun's own land.'

In the beginning of that winter a little son was born to Gudrid and Thorfinn.

'A health to the first Winelander!' the men shouted and drank down their wine; for they had made some from Wineland grapes.

'Will he be the father of a great country, as Ingolf was?' Biarni mused.

Gudrid looked at her baby and smiled.

'You will be as sunny as this good land, I hope,' she said.

They named him Snorri. He grew fast and soon crept along

the yellow sand, and toddled among the grapevines, and climbed into the boats and learned to talk. The men called him the 'Wineland king'.

'I never knew a baby before,' one of the men said.

'No,' said another. 'Swords are jealous. But when they are in their scabbards, we can do other things, even play with babies.'

'I wonder whether I have forgotten how to swing my sword in this quiet land,' another man said.

One spring morning when the men got up and went out from their huts to the fires to cook they saw a great many canoes in the harbour. Men were in them paddling toward shore.

'What is this?' cried the Norsemen to one another. 'Where did they come from? Are they foes? Who ever saw such boats before? The men's faces are brown.'

'Let every man have his sword ready,' cried Thorfinn. 'But do not draw until I command. Let us go to meet them.'

So they went and stood on the shore. Soon the men from the canoes landed and stood looking at the Norsemen. The strangers' skin was brown. Their faces were broad. Their hair was black. Their bodies were short. They wore leather clothes. One man among them seemed to be chief. He spread out his open hands to the Norsemen.

'He is showing us that he has no weapons,' Biarni said. 'He comes in peace.'

Then Thorfinn showed his empty hands and asked:

'What do you want?'

The stranger said something, but the Norsemen could not understand. It was some new language. Then the chief pointed to

one of the huts and walked toward it. He and his men walked all around it and felt of the timber and went into it and looked at all the things there – spades and cloaks and drinking-horns. As they looked they talked together. They went to all the other huts and looked at everything there. One of them found a red cloak. He spread it out and showed it to the others. They all stood about it and looked at it and felt of it and talked fast.

'They seem to like my cloak,' Biarni said.

One of the strangers went down to their canoes and soon came back with an armload of furs – fox-skins, otter-skins, beaver-skins. The chief took some and held them out to Thorfinn and hugged the cloak to him.

'He wants to trade,' Thorfinn said. 'Will you do it, Biarni?'

'Yes,' Biarni answered, and took the furs.

'If they want red stuff, I have a whole roll of red cloth that I will trade,' one of the other men said.

He went and got it. When the strangers saw it they quickly held out more furs and seemed eager to trade. So Thorfinn cut the cloth into pieces and sold every scrap. When the strangers got it they tied it about their heads and seemed much pleased.

While this trading was going on and everybody was good-natured, a bull of Thorfinn's ran out of the woods bellowing and came towards the crowd. When the strangers heard it and saw it they threw down whatever was in their hands and ran to their canoes and paddled off as fast as they could.

The Norsemen laughed.

'We have lost our customers,' Biarni said.

'Did they never see a bull before?' laughed one of the men.

'The chief held them out to Thorfinn and hugged the cloak to him'

Now after three weeks the Norsemen saw canoes in the bay again. This time it was black with them, there were so many. The people in them were all making a horrible shout.

'It is a war-cry,' Thorfinn said, and he raised a red shield. 'They are surely twenty to our one, but we must fight. Stand in close line and give them a taste of your swords.'

Even as he spoke a great shower of stones fell upon them. Some of the Norsemen were hit on the head and knocked down. Biarni got a broken arm. Still the storm came fast. The strangers had landed and were running toward the Norsemen. They threw their stones with sling-shots, and they yelled all the time.

'Oh, this is no kind of fighting for brave men!' Thorfinn cried angrily.

The Norsemen's swords swung fast, and many of the strangers died under them, but still others came on, throwing stones and swinging stone axes. The horrible yelling and the strange things that the savages did frightened the Norsemen.

'These are not men,' some one cried.

Then those Norsemen who had never been afraid of anything turned and ran. But when they came to the top of a rough hill Thorfinn cried:

'What are we doing? Shall we die here in this empty land with no one to bury us? We are leaving our women.'

Then one of the women ran out of the hut where they were hiding.

'Give me a sword!' she cried. 'I can drive them back. Are Norsemen not better than these savages?'

Then those warriors stopped, ashamed, and stood up before

the wild men and fought so fiercely that the strangers turned and fled down to their canoes and paddled away.

'Oh, I am glad they are gone!' Thorfinn said. 'It was an ugly fight.'

'Thor would not have loved that battle,' one said.

'It was no battle,' another replied. 'It was like fighting against an army of poisonous flies.'

The Norsemen were all worn and bleeding and sore. They went to their huts and dressed their wounds, and the women helped them. At supper that night they talked about the fight for a long time.

'I will not stay here,' Gudrid said. 'Perhaps these wild men have gone away to get more people and will come back and kill us. Oh! they are ugly.'

'Perhaps brown faces are looking at us now from behind the trees in the woods back there,' said Biarni.

It was the wish of all to go home. So after a few days they sailed back to Greenland with good weather all the way. The people at Eric's house were very glad to see them.

'We were afraid you had died,' they said.

'And I thought once that we should never leave Wineland alive,' Thorfinn answered.

Then they told all the story.

'I wonder why I had no such bad luck,' Leif said. 'But you have a better shipload than I got.'

He was looking at the bundles of furs and the kegs of wine.

'Yes,' said Thorfinn, 'we have come back richer than when we left. But I will never go again for all the skins in the woods.'

The next summer Thorfinn took Gudrid and Snorri and all his people and sailed back to Iceland, his home. There he lived until he died. People looked at him in wonder.

'That is the man who went to Wineland and fought with wild men,' they said. 'Snorri is his son. He is the first and last Winelander, for no one will ever go there again. It will be an empty and forgotten land.'

And so it was for a long time. Some wise men wrote down the story of those voyages and of that land, and people read the tale and liked it, but no one remembered where the place was. It all seemed like a fairy tale. Long afterwards, however, men began to read those stories with wide-open eyes and to wonder. They guessed and talked together, and studied this and that land, and read the story over and over. At last they have learned that Wineland was in America, on the eastern shore of the United States, and they have called Snorri the first American, and have put up statues of Leif Ericsson, the first comer to America.

The Saga of Thorstein, Viking's Son

I

The beginning of this Saga is, that a king named Loge ruled that country which is north of Norway. Loge was larger and stronger than any other man in that country. His name was lengthened from Loge to Haloge, and after him the country was called Halogeland (Halogaland, i.e. Haloge's land). Loge was the fairest of men, and his strength and stature was like unto that of his kinsmen, the giants, from whom he descended. His wife was Glod (Gloft, glad), a daughter of Grim of Grimsgard, which is situated in Jotunheim in the north; and Jotunheim was at that time called Elivags (Elivagar in the north). Grim was a very great berserk; his wife was Alvor, a sister of Alf the Old. He ruled that kingdom which lies between two rivers, both of which were called Elfs (i.e. Elbs), taking their name from him (Alf). The river south

of his kingdom, dividing it from Gautland, the country of King Gaut, was called Gaut's Elf (i.e. Gaut's River, the river Gotha in the southwestern part of the present Sweden); the one north of it was called Raum's Elf, named after King Raum, and the kingdom of the latter was called Raum's-ric. The land governed by King Alf was called Alfheim, and all his offspring are related to the Elves. They were fairer than any other people save the giants. King Alf was married to Bryngerd, a daughter of king Raum of Raum's-ric; she was a large woman, but she was not beautiful, because her father, king Raum, was ugly-looking, and hence ugly-looking and large men are called great 'raums'. King Haloge and his wife, queen Glod, had two daughters, named Eisa (glowing embers) and Eimyrja (embers). These maids were the fairest in the land, on account of their parentage, for their father and mother were both very fair. But as fire and light make dark things bright, so these things took their names from the above-named maids. There lived with Haloge two jarls, named Vifil and Vesete, both of whom were large and strong men, and they were the warders of the king's land. One day the jarls went to the king, Vifil to woo Eimyrja and Vesete to woo Eisa; but the king refused both, on which account they grew so angry that they soon afterward carried the maids off, fleeing with them out of the land, and thus putting themselves out of his reach. But the king declared them outlaws in his kingdom, hindered them by witchcraft from ever again becoming dwellers in his land, and, moreover, enchanted their kinsmen, making these also outlaws, and deprived them of the benefit of their estates forever. Vesete settled in an island or holm, which was called Borgund's holm (Bornholm), and became

the father of Bue and Sigurd, nicknamed Cape. Vifil sailed further to the east and established himself in an island called Vifil's Isle. With his wife, Eimyrja, he got a son, Viking by name, who in his early youth became a man of great stature and extraordinary strength.

II

THERE was a king named Ring, who ruled a fylke of Sweden. With his queen he had an only child, a daughter, by name Hunvor, a maiden of unrivalled beauty and education. She had a magnificent bower, and was attended by a suite of maidens. Ingeborg named the maiden, who was next to her in position, and she was a daughter of Herfinn, jarl of Woollen Acre. Most people said that Ingeborg was not inferior to the daughter of the king in any respect, excepting in strength and wisdom, which Hunvor possessed in a higher degree than all others in the land. Many kings and princes wooed Ingeborg, but she refused them all. She was thought to be a woman of boundless pride and insolence, and it was also talked by many that her pride and insolence might some day receive a check in some way or other. Thus time passed on for a while. There was a mountain back of the king's residence so high that no human paths traversed it. One day a man – if he might be so called – came down from the mountain. He was larger and more fierce-looking than any person that had before been seen, and he looked more like a giant than like a human being. In his hand he held a bayonet-like two-pointed pike. This happened while the king was sitting at the table. This 'raum' (ugly-looking fellow) came to the door of the hall and requested to be permitted to enter, but the porters refused to admit him. Then he smote the porters with his pike and pierced both of them from breast to back, one being pierced by one point of the pike and the other by the other; whereupon he lifted both of them over his head and threw their corpses down upon the ground behind him. Then, entering the door, he approached the king's throne, and thus addressed him: 'As I, king Ring, have honoured you so much as to visit you, I think it your duty to grant my request.' The king asked what the request might be, and what his name was. He answered: 'My name is Harek, the Ironhead, and I am a son of king Kol Kroppinbak (the humpback) of India; but my errand is that I wish you to place your daughter, your country, and your subjects in my hands. And, I think, most people will say that it is better for the kingdom that I rule it instead of you, who are destitute of strength and manhood, and, moreover, enfeebled by age. But, as it may seem humiliating to you to surrender your kingdom, I will agree, on my part, to marry your daughter, Hunvor. But, if this is not satisfactory to you, I will kill you, take possession of your kingdom, and make Hunvor my concubine.' Now the king felt sorely perplexed, for all the people were grieved at their conversation. Then said the king: 'It seems to me that we ought to know what she will answer.' To this Harek assented. Then Hunvor was sent for, and the matter was explained to her. She said: 'I like the looks of this man very well, although he seems likely to treat me with severity; but I consider him perfectly worthy of me, if I marry him; nevertheless, I wish to ask whether no ransom can be paid and I be free.' 'Yes, there can, answered Harek. If the king will

try a holm-gang with me within four nights, or procure another man in his stead, then all powers shall be surrendered to the one slaying the other in the duel.' 'Certainly,' answered Hunvor, 'none can be found who is able to subdue you in a duel; nevertheless, I will agree to your proposition.' After this, Harek went out, but Hunvor betook herself to her bower, weeping bitterly. Then the king asked his men if there was nobody among them who regarded his daughter Hunvor a sufficient prize for which to risk his life in a holm-gang with Harek. But, although all wished to marry her, yet nobody was willing to risk the duel, looking upon it as certain death. Many also said that this fate was deserved by her, since she had refused so many, and marrying Harek would be a check to her pride. She had a man-servant, by name Eymund, a fellow faithful to her and to be trusted in all matters. This man she sent for straightway on the same day, saying to him: 'It will not prove advisable to keep quiet; I want to send you away; take a boat and row to the island, which lies outside of Woollen Acre, and is called Vifil's Isle. On the island there is a byre (farm, farm-house); thither you must go and arrive there tomorrow at nightfall. You are to enter the western door of the byre, and when you have entered you will see a sprightly old man and an elderly woman; any other persons you will not see. They have a son by name Viking, who is now fifteen years old and a man of great ability, but he will not be present. I hope he will be able to help us out of our troubles; if not, I fear there will scarcely be any help for us. You must keep out of sight, but if you happen to see a third person, then throw this letter on his lap and hurry home.' Without delay, Eymund, with a company of eleven men, went on board a ship and sailed to

Vifil's Isle. He goes ashore alone and proceeds to the byre, where he finds the fire-house and places himself behind the door. The bonde (farmer) was sitting by the fire with his wife, and he seemed to Eymund a man of brave countenance. The fire was almost burnt out and the house was but faintly lighted by the embers. Said the woman: 'I think, my dear Vifil, that it would prove to our advantage if our son Viking should present himself, for no one seems to be offering himself for combat, and the time for the duel with Harek is close at hand.' 'I do not think it advisable, Eimyrja, answered he, for our son is yet young and rash, ambitious and careless. It will be his sudden death if he should be induced to fight with Harek; nevertheless, it is for you to manage this matter as you think best.' Presently a door opened back of the bonde, and a man of wonderful stature entered, taking his seat by the side of his mother. Eymund threw the letter on the lap of Viking, ran to the ship, came to Hunvor and told her how he had done his errand. 'Fate will now have to settle the matter,' said Hunvor. Viking took the letter, in which he found a greeting from the king's daughter, and, moreover, a promise that she would be his wife if he would fight with Harek, the Ironhead. At this Viking turned pale, observing which, Vifil asked him what letter that was. Viking showed him the letter. 'This I knew,' said Vifil, 'and it would have been better, Eimyrja, if I had decided this matter myself, when we talked about it a little while ago, but what do you propose to do?' Said Viking: 'Would it not be well to save the princess?' Replied Vifil: 'It will be sudden death to you if you fight with Harek.' 'I will run the risk, answered Viking.' 'Then there is no remedy,' said Vifil, 'but I will give you an account of his family and of himself.

III

TIRUS THE GREAT was king of India. He was an excellent ruler in every respect, and his queen was a very superior woman, with whom, he had an only daughter, who was named Trona. She was the fairest among the fair, and, unlike the majority of her sex, she excelled all other princesses in wisdom. The Saga must also mention a man by name Kol, of whom a great many good things are told: first, that he was large as a giant, ugly-looking as the devil, and so well skilled in the black art that he could pass through the earth as well as walk upon it, could glue together steeds and stars; furthermore, he was so great a ham-leaper[1] that he could burst into the shape of various kinds of animals; he would sometimes ride on the winds or pass through the sea, and he had so large a hump on his back that, although he stood upright, the hump would reach above his head. This Kol went to India with a great army, slew Tirus, married Trona, and subjugated the land and the people. He begot many children with Trona, all of whom were more like their father than like their mother. Kol was nicknamed Kroppinbak (i.e. Humpback). He had three rare treasures. These were: a sword so mighty that none better was wielded at that time, and the name of this sword was Angervadil; another of the treasures was a gold ring, called Gleser; the third was a horn, and such was the nature of the beverage contained in the lower part of it that all who drank therefrom were attacked by an illness called leprosy, and became

[1] Ham-leaper, one who is able to change his shape.

so forgetful that they remembered nothing of the past; but by drinking from the upper part of the horn their health and memory were restored. Their eldest child was Bjorn, the Blue-tooth. His tooth was of a blue colour, and extended an ell and a half out of his mouth; with this tooth he often, in battles or when he was violently in rage, put people to death. A daughter of Kol was Dis. The third child of Kol and Trona was named Harek, whose head at the age of seven was perfectly bald, and whose skull was as hard as steel, wherefore he was called Ironhead. Their fourth child was named Ingjald, whose upper lip measured an ell from the nose, whence he was called Ingjald Trana (the snout). It was the pastime of the brothers when at home that Bjorn the Blue-tooth cut his tooth into the skull of his brother Harek with all his might without hurting him. No weapon could be made to stick in the lip of Ingjald Snout. By incantations Kol the Hump-back brought it about, that none of his offspring could be killed by any other weapon than by the sword Angervadil; no other iron can scathe them. But when Kol had become old enough he died a horrible death. At the time of his death Trona was pregnant, and gave birth to a son, called Kol after his father, and he was as like his father as he was akin to him. One year old, Kol was so ugly to children that he was nicknamed Kol Krappe (the crafty). Dis married Jokul Ironback, a blue berserk. She and her brothers divided their father's heritage betwixt themselves, so that Dis got the horn, but Bjorn Bluetooth the sword, Harek the ring, Ingjald the kingdom, and Kol the personal property. Three winters after the death of king Kol, Trona married jarl Herfinn, a son of king Rodmar of Marseraland, and the first winter after

they were married she bore him a son, named Framar, who was a man of great possibilities and unlike his brothers. 'Now it seems to me,' continued Vifil, 'that you ought not to risk your life in a duel with this Hel-strong man, whom no iron can scathe.' 'Not so, answered Viking; I shall run the risk, whatsoever may be the result.' And Vifil, seeing that Viking was in real earnest when he insisted on fighting with Harek, said: 'I can tell you still more about the sons of Kol. Vesete and I were wardens of king Haloge's country; during the summer seasons we used to wage wars, and once we met Bjorn Blue-tooth in Grening's Sound (the present Gronsund, between the Isle of Man and Falster in Denmark), and in such a manner did we fight that Vesete smote Bjorn's hand with his club, so that the sword fell from his hand, and then I caught it, flung it through him, and he lost his life. From that time I have worn the sword, and now I give it to you, my son.' Vifil then brought forth the sword and gave it to Viking, who liked it very much. Viking then prepared himself, went on board a boat, and came to the hall of the king on the day appointed for the duel. There everything was sad and dreary. Viking went before the king and greeted him. The king asked him his name. Viking told him the truth. Hunvor was sitting on one side of the king. Then Viking asked her whether she had requested him to come. She replied in the affirmative. Viking asked what terms he offered him for venturing a holm-gang with Harek. Replied the king: 'I will give you my daughter in marriage, and a suitable dowry besides.' Viking gave his consent to this, and then he was betrothed to Hunvor; but it was the common opinion that it would be certain death to him if he should fight with Harek.

IV

THEN Viking went to the holm, accompanied by the king and his courtiers. Thither came Harek, too, and asked who was appointed to fight with him. Viking stepped forward and said: 'I am the man.' Whereto Harek made reply: 'I suppose it will be an easy matter to strike you to the ground, for I know it will be the end of you if I smite you with my fist.' 'But I suppose, answered Viking, that you consider it no trifling matter to fight with me, since you tremble at the very sight of me.' Harek replies: 'Not so, and I must save your life, since you go willingly into the open jaws of death; and do you smite first, according to the laws of holm-gang, for I am the challenger in this duel; but, in the meantime, I shall stand perfectly still, for I am not afraid of any danger.' At this time Viking drew his sword, Angervadil, from which lightning seemed to flash. Harek seeing this, said: 'I would never have fought with you had I known that you were in possession of Angervadil, and most likely it will turn out as my father said, namely, that I and my brothers and my sister would all be short-lived, excepting the one bearing his own name, and it was a great misfortune that Angervadil passed out of the hands of our family.' At this moment Viking struck Harek's skull and split his trunk from one end to the other, so that the sword stood in the ground to the hilt. Then the men of the king burst out in loud triumphant shouting, and the king went home to his hall with great joy. Now they began to talk about preparing the wedding-feast, but Viking said he was not willing to be married yet; she shall remain betrothed, he said, and not be wedded till after three years, meanwhile I am going to

wage war. So was done, and Viking went abroad with two ships. He was very successful, gaining victory in every battle; and after having spent two years as a viking, he landed at an island in the autumn at a time when the weather was fair and very warm.

V

THE same day as Viking landed at the island, he went ashore to amuse himself. He turned his steps to a forest and then he grew very hot. Having come to an open place in the forest, he sat down, and saw a woman of exquisite beauty walking along. She came up to him, greeted him very courteously, and he received her very kindly. They talked together a long time, and their conversation was very friendly. He asked her her name, and she said it was Solbjort (sun-bright). She then asked him if he was not thirsty, as he had walked so far, but Viking said he was not. She then took a horn, which she had kept under her cloak, offered him a drink from it, and he accepting it, and drinking therefrom, became sleepy, and bending his body into the lap of Solbjort, he fell asleep. But when he woke up again she had entirely disappeared. The drink had made him feel somewhat strange, and his whole body was shivering; the weather was gusty and cold, and he had forgotten nearly everything of the past, and least of all did he recollect Hunvor. He then went to his ship and departed from that place, and now he was confined to his bed by the disease called leprosy. He and his men frequently sailed near land, but were unwilling to go ashore and remain there. After having suffered twelve months from this sickness it grew still more severe, and his body was covered with many sores. One day sailing to land, they saw three ships passing the harbour, and at their meeting they asked for each other's names. Viking told his name, but the other chieftain said his name was Halfdan, and that he was a son of Ulf. Halfdan was a large and strong-looking man, and when he had learned the condition of Viking he went on board his ship, where he found him very weak. Halfdan asked him the cause of his illness, and Viking told him everything that had happened. Halfdan answered: 'Here the ham-leaper, Dis, Kol's daughter, has succeeded in her tricks, and I think it will be difficult to get any assistance from her in righting this matter, for she undoubtedly thinks she has avenged her brother, Harek Ironhead. Now I will offer you foster-brotherhood, and we will try whether we cannot revenge ourselves on Dis.' Answered Viking to this: 'Owing to my weakness, I have no hope at all of being able to kill Dis and her husband, Jokul Ironback, but such is my opinion of you, that even though I were in the best circumstances, your valour makes your offer very flattering to me.' And thus it was agreed that they should become foster-brothers. Halfdan had a great dragon, called Iron-ram; all of this ship that stood out of the water was ironclad; it rose high out of the sea, and was a very costly treasure. Having spent a short time there they left the place and went home to Svafe. Then Viking's strength diminished so that he became sick unto death. But when they had landed, Halfdan left the ships alone and proceeded until he came into an open space in a forest, where there stood a large rock, which he went up to and knocked at with his rod, and out of the rock there came a dwarf, who lived there

and was named Lit (colour), a warm friend of Halfdan, whom the dwarf greeted kindly and asked what his errand was. Replied Halfdan: 'It is now of great importance to me, foster-father, that you do my errand.' 'What is it, my foster-son?' asked Lit. 'I want you to procure for me the good horn of Dis, Kol's daughter,' said Halfdan. 'Risk that yourself,' said Lit, 'for it will be my death if I attempt it; and even the sacrifice of myself would be in vain, for you know there does not exist such a troll in the whole world as Dis.' Replied Halfdan: 'I am sure you will do as well as you can.' Upon this they parted, Halfdan returning to his ships and remaining there for some time.

VI

NOW it must be told of king Ring that he and his daughter Hunvor dwelt in his kingdom after the slaying of Harek Ironhead, which seemed to all a deed of great daring. This event was heard of in India, and Ingjald Snout was startled by the tidings of Harek's death. He began to cut the war-arrow, and dispatched it throughout the whole country, thus collecting an army containing a crowd of people, among whom there were many of the rabble, and with this army he marched toward Sweden. He came there unexpected, and offered the king battle. The challenge was accepted without delay, although the king had but a few men, and the result of this battle was soon decided. King Ring fell, together with all his courtiers; but Ingjald took Hunvor and Ingeborg and carried them away to India. Jokul Ironback went to seek after the foster-brothers, wishing to revenge the death of his brother-in-law, Harek. Now the story goes on to tell about Viking and Halfdan staying at Svafe. Seven nights had passed away when Lit met Halfdan and brought the horn to him. This made Halfdan very glad, and he went to Viking, whom almost everybody then thought to be not far from death. Halfdan put a drop of fluid from the upper part of the horn on Viking's lips. This brought Viking to his senses; he began to grow stronger and was like unto a person awakening from a slumber; and the uncleanness fell from him as scales fall from a fish. Thus he, day by day, grew better and was restored. After this they got ready to depart from Svafe, and directed their course north of Balegard-side. There they saw eighteen ships, all of large size and covered with black tents. Said Halfdan: 'Here I think Jokul Ironback and his wife, the ham-leaper, are lying before us, and I do not know how Lit has parted with them, he being so exhausted that he could not speak. But now I think there is good reason for going to battle. Let everything of value be taken away from the ships, and let stones be put in instead.' This was done. Then after a quick rowing to the strangers, they asked who the chieftains were. Jokul gave them his name and asked for their names in return. They said they were named Halfdan and Viking. Then we need not ask what came to pass. A very hot battle took place, and the foster-brothers lost more men than Jokul, for the latter dealt heavy blows. Then Viking, followed by Halfdan, made an attempt to board Jokul's dragon, after which a great number of the crew of the dragon were slain. Jokul and Halfdan met and exchanged blows with each other; but although Jokul was the stronger, Halfdan succeeded in giving him a blow across the

back with his sword; yet, in spite of his being without his coat-of-mail, the sword did not scathe him. Meanwhile Viking came to Halfdan's assistance. He smote Jokul's shoulder and split his side, thus separating one arm and both feet, the one above the knee, from the trunk. Then Jokul fell, but was not yet dead, and said: 'I knew that when Dis had been forsaken by luck, much of evil was in store; the first of all was that the villain Lit betrayed her, and thus succeeded by tricks in stealing the horn from her and at the same time hurt her, so that she is still confined to her bed from the encounter; but I should also be inclined to think that he has not escaped without some injury himself either. Had she been on foot, the matter would not have resulted thus. But I am glad you have not got the princess Hunvor from my brother-in-law, Ingjald Snout.' After this he soon died, and then a cry of victory was shouted and quarter was given to the wounded who could be cured. They got much booty there, and on shore they found Dis almost lifeless from the encounter with Lit. Her they seized, put a belg (whole skin) over her head, and stoned her to death. Hereupon they went back to Svafe and cured the wounds of their men. And having equipped twenty-four ships, all well furnished with men and weapons, they announced that they were bound for India.

VII

INGJALD SNOUT made great preparations, fortifying the walls of his burg (town, city) and collecting a great number of people, some of which were rabble of the worst kind. As soon as the foster-brothers had landed they harried the country with fire and sword; everybody was in fear of them, and before Ingjald was aware of it they had made a great plunder. Now he goes against them; they met, and a battle was fought. Halfdan and Viking thought they had never before been in so great danger as in this battle. The foster-brothers showed great bravery, and toward the end of the battle more men began to fall in Ingjald's army. The battle lasted four days, and at last none but Ingjald remained on his feet. He could not be wounded at all, and seemed to move through the air as easily as on the ground. Finally, by surrounding him with shields, they succeeded in getting him captive, put him in chains, and bound his hands with a bow-string. It was then so dark that they did not think it convenient to kill him on the spot, Viking being unwilling to slay a man at night-time. They ran into the burg and carried Hunvor and Ingeborg away to their ships. Here they lay during the night; but in the morning the warders were dead, and Ingjald was not to be found, his chains lying unbroken and the bow-string not untied. No mark of iron could be found on the warders, and thus it was clear that Ingjald had made use of troll-craft. Now they hoisted their sails, left this country, and directed their course homeward to Sweden. Then Viking made preparations for the wedding, and married Hunvor. At the same time Halfdan began his suit and asked for the hand of Ingeborg, the daughter of the jarl. Word was sent to jarl Herfinn of Woollen Acre. He came and gave a favourable answer, and it was agreed that Halfdan should marry Ingeborg. Arrangements for the wedding were made, and the marriage ceremony was performed. The foster-

brothers stayed there during the winter. The following summer they went abroad with ten ships, waged wars in the Baltic, and having got great booty they returned home in the autumn. Thus they lived as vikings three years, spending only the winters at home; and none were more famous than they. One summer they sailed to Denmark; here they harried and entered the Limfjord, where they saw nine ships and a dragon lying at anchor. They immediately directed their fleet toward these ships, and asked for the name of the commander. He said he was called Njorfe, and added: 'I am the ruler of the Uplands in Norway, and I have just gotten my paternal heritage; but what is the name of those who have just come?' They told him this. Said Halfdan: 'I will offer to you, as to other vikings, two conditions: the one that you give up your fee, ships and weapons, and go ashore free; and the other, that you fight a battle with us.' Answered Njorfe: 'This seems to me hard terms, and I choose rather to defend my fee, and, if need be, fall with bravery, than to flee feeless and dishonoured, although you have a larger army and ships of greater size and number than mine.' Said Viking: 'We shall not be so mean as to attack you with more ships than you have; five of our ships shall therefore lie idle during the battle.' Answered Njorfe: 'This is bravely spoken.' And so they got ready for the battle, which then began. They fought with their ships stem to stem. The attack was very violent on both sides, for Njorfe fought with great daring, and the foster-brothers also showed great bravery. Three days they fought, but still they did not seem to know who would win. Asked then Viking: 'Is there much fee in your ships?' Answered Njorfe: 'No, for from those places where we have been harrying this summer the bondes fled with their fee, and hence but little booty has been taken.' Said Viking: 'Unwise it seems to me to fight only for the sake of outdoing each other, and thus spill the blood of many men; but are you willing to form a league with us?' Answered Njorfe: 'It will be good for me to form a league with you, although you are not a king's son, for I know that your father was a jarl, and an excellent man; and I am willing to have a foster-brotherhood formed between us on the condition that you are named jarl and I king, according to our birth-right, which must remain unchanged whether we are in my kingdom or in any other.' During this talk Halfdan was silent. Viking asked why he had so little to say in this matter. Answered Halfdan: 'It seems to me that it may be good to make such an agreement betwixt you; but I shall not be surprised if you should get to feel that some or other of Njorfe's relatives become burdensome to you. I will, however, have nothing to do with this matter – will neither dissuade nor encourage you.' The result was, that Njorfe and Viking came to terms and formed a foster-brotherhood, giving oaths mutually on the terms which have before been stated. They waged wars during the summer and took much booty; but in the autumn they parted, Njorfe going to Norway, and Viking, accompanied by Halfdan, to Sweden. But soon after Viking had come home, Hunvor was taken sick and died. They had a son, who was called Ring. He was brought up in Sweden until he was full-grown, and became a king of that country. He did not live long, but had a great many descendants. The foster-brothers kept on waging wars every summer and became very famous; during their warfares they gathered so many ships that they had fifty in all.

VIII

IT must be told of Ingjald Snout, that he gathered an innumerable army and went to search for the foster-brothers, Viking and Halfdan. And one summer they met in the Baltic, Ingjald having forty ships. It came straightway to a fight, and they fought in such a manner that it was not easy to see which side would win. At last Viking, immediately followed by Njorfe and Halfdan, tried to board Ingjald's dragon. They made a great havoc, killing one man after the other. Then Ingjald rushed toward the stern of the dragon, with a great atgeir (a kind of javelin) ready for slaughter. Now the foster-brothers attacked Ingjald, and although they fought a large part of the day with him they did not wound him, and when the fight seemed to Ingjald to grow very hot, he sprang overboard, followed by Njorfe and Halfdan, both swimming as fast as they could. Viking did not stop fighting before he had slain every man on the dragon, after which he jumped into a boat and rowed ashore. Ingjald kept swimming till he reached the land, and then Halfdan and Njorfe were drawing near to the surf. Ingjald took a stone and threw it at Halfdan, but he dodged under the water. Meanwhile Njorfe landed, and Halfdan soon after him, in another place. They attacked Ingjald mightily, and having fought thus for a long time, they heard a great crash, and looked thither whence they heard the crash, but on turning their faces back, Ingjald was out of sight, and instead of him there was a grim-looking boar, that left nothing undone as he attacked them, so they could do nothing but defend themselves. When this had been done for some time, the boar turned upon Halfdan, bearing away the whole calf of his leg. Straightway came Viking and smote the bristles of the boar, so that his back was cut in two. Then seeing that Ingjald lay dead on the spot, they kindled a fire and burned him to ashes. Now they went back to their ships and bound up the wounds of Halfdan. After this they sailed away from this place north to an isle called Thruma, and ruled by a man named Refil a son of the sea-king Mefil. He had a daughter named Finna, a maid of surpassing fairness and accomplishments. Viking courted her, and with king Njorfe's help, and Halfdan's bravery, the marriage was agreed to. Then the foster-brothers ended their warfaring. King Njorfe established himself in his kingdom, and Viking took his abode with him and became his jarl, but Halfdan was made a great herser and dwelt on his byre, called Vags. His land was separated by a mountain from that which was ruled by jarl Viking. They held to their friendship as long as they lived, but it was more cold between Halfdan and Njorfe.

IX

A KING, named Olaf, ruled Fjord-fylke (the county of the fjords). He was a son of Eystein and a brother of Onund, who was the father of Ingjald the Wicked. They were all unsafe and wicked in their dealings. King Olaf had a daughter called Bryngerd, whom Njorfe married, took her with him, and got with her nine sons: Jokul was the eldest of these brothers; the rest were named Olaf, Grim, Geiter, Teit, Tyrfing, Bjorn, Geir, Grane and Toke. They were all promising men, though Jokul far surpassed them

all in all accomplishments. He was so haughty that he thought everything below himself. Olaf stood next to him, as a man skilful in all deeds; but he was of a noisy, troublesome and overbearing temperament, and the same might be said of all his brothers, and they boasted very much. Viking had nine sons, the eldest of whom was Thorstein, and the others were called Thorer, Finn, Ulf, Stein, Romund, Finnboge, Eystein and Thorgeir. They were hopeful men, of great skill in action, though Thorstein held the highest rank among them in everything. He was the largest and strongest of men; he was popular, steadfast in his friendship, faithful and reliable in all things. He could not easily be provoked to do harm, but when attacked he revenged himself grimly. If he was insulted, it could scarcely be seen in his daily life whether he liked it or not, but long afterward he would act as if he had just been injured. Thorer was of a most sanguine and vehement temperament; if injured or affronted he would suddenly be seized by an irresistible rage, and, no matter whom he had to do with, or what the result might be, he never hesitated to do whatsoever came into his mind. He was a most adroit man in all kinds of games, and a man of uncommon strength. He was second only to his brother Thorstein. These young men grew up together in the kingdom. In the mountain separating Viking's and Halfdan's lands, there was a chasm of fearful depth and of a breadth of thirty ells at the narrowest, so that it was perfectly impassable for human beings, and hence the mountain was not crossed by any paths. It had been tried by king Njorfe and jarl Viking and Halfdan how easily they might leap over the chasm. The result was, that Viking had leaped over it in full armour, Njorfe had done it in his lightest clothes, but Halfdan had only done it by being received on the other side by Viking. Now they all kept quiet for a long time, and the friendship of jarl Viking and king Njorfe remained unimpaired.

X

AT NJORFE and Viking became old, and their sons were rapidly advancing in growth. Jokul became in all things a violent and restless man. The sons of Njorfe were of nearly the same age as the sons of Viking, the youngest ones being at this point of our Saga about twelve years old, while Thorstein and Jokul were at the age of twenty. The sons of Njorfe used to play with the sons of Viking, and the latter were in no way below the former. This made the sons of the king very jealous, and in their jealousy, as in all other things, Jokul surpassed all; and it was easy to see that Thorstein yielded to Jokul in all things, nor was this any reproach to him. Thorstein far surpassed all his brothers and all other men known. Jarl Viking had warned his sons not to vie with the sons of the king in any games, but rather to spare their strength and eagerness. One day the king's sons and the sons of Viking were playing ball, and the game was played very eagerly by the sons of Njorfe. Thorstein, as usual, checked his zeal. He was placed against Jokul, and Thorer was placed against Olaf, and the others were placed in the same manner, according to their age. Thus the day was spent. It happened that Thorer threw the ball on the ground so hard that it bounded over Olaf and fell down again far off. At this Olaf turned angry, thinking that Thorer was mocking

him. He fetched the ball; but when he came back the game was being broken up, and the people were going home. Olaf then with the ball-club struck after Thorer, who, seeing it, dodged the blow in such a manner that the club touched his head and wounded it. But Thorstein, together with many other people, hurried betwixt them and parted them. Said Jokul: 'I suppose you think it a thing of no great weight that Thorer got a bump on his head.' Thorer blushed at Jokul's words, and thus they parted. Said Thorer then: 'I have left my gloves behind, and if I do not fetch them Jokul will lay it to my fear.' Answered Thorstein: 'I do not think it advisable that you and Olaf meet.' 'Nevertheless I will go,' said Thorer, 'for they have gone home.' So saying, he turned back at a swinging pace, and when he came to the play-ground everybody had left it. Then Thorer turned his steps toward the hall of the king. At the same moment the sons of the king also came home to the hall, and stood near the wall of the hall. Then Thorer turned toward Olaf and stabbed his waist, so that the spear passed through his body; whereupon he withdrew and escaped out of their hands. They, on the other hand, had a great ado over Olaf's corpse; but Thorer went until he found his brother. Now asked him Thorstein: 'Why is there blood on your spear, brother?' Answered Thorer: 'Because I do not know whether Olaf has not perhaps been wounded by the point of it.' Said Thorstein: 'You perhaps tell of his death.' Quoth Thorer: 'It may be that Jokul will not be able to heal the wound of his brother Olaf, though he be a very skilful man in almost all things.' Answered Thorstein: 'This is a sorry thing that now has happened; for I know that my father will dislike it.' And when they came home jarl Viking was out-doors, and looked very stern. Said he: 'What I looked for from you, Thorer, has now come to pass, that you would be the most luck-forsaken of all my sons. This you have shown, as I think, by killing the son of the king himself.' Answered Thorstein: 'Now is the time, father, to help your son, although he has fallen into ill-luck; and that you know means for this purpose I think you have shown by your being aware of Olaf's death while nobody had told you of it.' Answered Viking: 'I am unwilling to sacrifice so much as to break my oaths for the life of Thorer; for both of us, king Njorfe and I, have sworn to be faithful and trusty to each other, both in private and public matters. These oaths he has kept in all matters. Now I will not, therefore, show myself worse than he has been; but this I would do if I should fight against him, for there was a time when king Njorfe was as dear to me as my own sons, and it needs not be hinted at that I should give Thorer any help; he must leave, and never more come before my eyes.' Answered Thorstein: 'Why should not all of us brothers then leave home? for we will not part with Thorer, but stand by one another for weal or for woe.' Answered the jarl: 'That is a matter that rests with you, my son; but great I must call the ill-luck of Thorer, if he is to be the cause of my losing all my sons and my friendship with the king too, who is the doughtiest man in all things, and besides these, my life, which is, however, worth but little. But there is one thing that makes me glad, and that is that it will not fall to the lot of any one to put you to death, although your escape will be narrow enough, and this will all be caused by Thorer's ill-luck; nevertheless, the loss of him will be felt on account of his valour. Now, my son Thorstein, here is a sword, which I will give to you; Angervadil is its name, and it has

always had victory with it; my father took it from Bjorn Bluetooth at his death. I have no other distinguished weapons except an old kesia, which I took from Harek Ironhead; but I know that nobody is able to wield it as a weapon. Now if you are going to leave home, my son Thorstein, then it is my advice that you go up to a lake named Vener; there you will find a boat belonging to me, standing in a boat-house; go in it to a holm which lies in the lake; there you will find in a shed food and clothes enough to last you twelve months; take good care of the boat, for there are no more ships in the neighbourhood.' Hereupon the brothers parted with their father. The brothers all had good clothes and armour, which had been given them by their father before this happened. Thorstein and his brothers went until they found the boat. Then they rowed to the holm, and found the shed; here was enough of all things which they needed, and they took up their abode there.

XI

NOW it is to be told that Jokul and his brothers told of the death of Olaf to their father. Said Jokul: 'This is the only thing to be done, that we bring together an army and march to the house of Viking and burn him and all his sons alive in their house, and even this would scarcely be vengeance enough for Olaf's death.' Said Njorfe: 'I wholly forbid that any harm be done to Viking, for I know that my son has not been slain by his advice, and no one is guilty of this but Thorer. But Viking and I have sworn to each other an oath of brotherhood, and this oath he has kept better than anyone else, and hence I shall not wage any war against him, for I do not think Olaf will be atoned for in the least by slaying Thorer, and thus giving more grief to Viking.' And so Jokul did not get any help in this matter from his father. Olaf was buried with the usual ceremonies of olden times, and from this time Jokul began to keep a suite of men. King Njorfe was already growing very old, so that Jokul for the most part had to ward the land. One day it happened that two men went before Njorfe, both dressed in blue frocks. They greeted the king. He asked them for their names. One of them said he was called Gautan, the other said his name was Ogautan, and they bade the king give them winter quarter. Answered the king: 'To me you look ugly, and I will not receive you.' Said Jokul: 'Have you any accomplishments?' Answered Ogautan: 'As to that, we have not much to boast of; still we know many more things than people have spoken to us about.' Said Jokul: 'It seems best to me then that you enter my suite and stay with me.' So they did. Jokul did well by them. It had been heard at the king's hall that Viking had banished his sons. Jokul was unwilling to believe it, and went to Viking with a large suite. Viking asked what his errand was, and Jokul asked him what he knew about the miscreant Thorer. Viking told him that he had banished his sons, so that they did not live there. Jokul asked to be allowed to search the rooms of the house. Viking granted this, but said the king would not have thought that he would deceive him. They then searched the rooms, but, as might be expected, found nothing; and having done this they returned home. Jokul did not like that he heard nothing of the brothers, and so he said to Ogautan and his comrade: 'Would not you by your cunning be able to find out where the brothers have their dwelling-place?'

'I guess not,' answered Ogautan; 'you are nevertheless to let me and my brother have a house to sleep in, and nobody must come there before you, nor must you visit the house until after three days.' Jokul saw that this was done, and a small separate house was assigned for them to sleep in. Jokul positively forbade all people mentioning them, and he threatened the transgressor of his orders with certain death. Early on the day agreed upon Jokul came to the house of the brothers. Said then Ogautan: 'You are too hasty, Jokul, for I have just awaked; still I can tell you about the sons of Viking. You know, I suppose, where there is a lake called Vener. In it is a holm, and on the holm a shed, and there are the sons of Viking.' Answered Jokul: 'If what you say is so, then I have no hope of their being overtaken.' Said Ogautan: 'In all things you seem to me to act like a motherless child, and I do not think you will be able to do much alone. Now I will tell you,' continued Ogautan, 'that I have a belg (skin-bag) called the weatherbelg. If I shake it, storm and wind will blow out of it, together with such biting frost and cold that within three nights the lake shall be covered with so strong an ice that you may cross it on horseback if you wish.' Said Jokul: 'Really you are a man of great cunning; and this is the only way of reaching the holm, for there are no ships before you get to the sea, and nobody can carry them so far.' Hereupon Ogautan took his belg and shook it, and out of it there came so fearful a snowstorm and such biting frost that nobody could be out of doors. This was a thing of great wonder to all; and after three nights every water and fjord was frozen. Then Jokul gathered together men to the number of thirty. King Njorfe did not like this journey, and said his mind told him it would cause him more and not less sorrow;

for in this journey, he said, 'I will lose the most of my sons and a great many other men. It would have been better if we, according to my will in the beginning, had come to terms with Thorer, and thus kept the friendship of jarl Viking and his sons.'

XII

NOW Jokul got himself ready for the journey together with his thirty men, and besides them Gautan and Ogautan. The same morning Thorstein awoke in his shed and said: 'Are you awake, Thorer?' Answered he: 'I am, but I have been sleeping until now.' Said Thorstein: 'It is my will that we get ourselves ready for leaving the shed, for I know that Jokul will come here today together with many men.' Answered Thorer: 'I do not think so, and I am unwilling to go at all; or have you any sign of this?' 'I dreamt,' said Thorstein, 'that twenty-two wolves were running hither, and besides them there were seven bears, and the eighth one, a red-cheeked bear, large and grim-looking. And besides these there were two she-foxes leading the party; the latter were very ugly-looking, and seemed to me the most disgusting of all. All the wolves attacked us, and at last they seemed to tear to pieces all my brothers excepting you alone, and yet you fell. Many of the bears we slew, and all the wolves I killed, and the smaller one of the foxes, but then I fell.' Asked Thorer: 'What do you think this dream means?' Made answer Thorstein: 'I think that the large red-cheeked bear must be the fylgia (follower, guardian-spirit) of Jokul, and the other bears the fylgias of his brothers; but the wolves

undoubtedly were, to my mind, as many as the men who came with them; for, certainly they are wolfishly-minded toward us. But besides them there were two she-foxes, and I do not know any men to whom such fylgias belong; I therefore suppose that some persons hated by almost everybody have lately come to Jokul, and thus these fylgias may belong to them. Now, I have told you this my thought about the matter, and we will have to act in the manner pointed out to me in my sleep, and I would that we might avoid all trouble.' Said Thorer: 'I think your dream has been nothing but a scare-crow and idle forebodings, still it would not be uninteresting to try our mutual strength.' Quoth Thorstein: 'I do not think so; it seems to me that an unequal meeting is intended, and I should like that we might get ready to go away from here. Thorer said he would not go away, and it had to be as he would have it.' Thorstein arose and took his weapons, and all his brothers did likewise, but Thorer was very slow about it. At the very time when they had gotten themselves ready, Jokul came up with his men. The shed had two doors, one of which Thorstein guarded together with three of his brothers, the other was guarded by Thorer together with four men. A sharp attack then began; the brothers warded themselves bravely, but Jokul attacked the door warded by Thorer so strongly that three of his brothers fell, but one of them was driven out of the door to the spot where Thorstein stood. Thorer still guarded the door for a while, being by no means willing to yield. Then he turned out of the door and found his way among the enemies down upon the ice. They surrounded him, but he defended himself very bravely. Thorstein seeing this, ran out of the shed together with those of his brothers who were yet alive, went down onto the ice where Thorer was standing, and now a fierce combat took place. Thorstein and Thorer dealt many heavy blows, and at last all the brothers had fallen excepting Thorstein and Thorer; and all the sons of Njorfe had also fallen save Jokul and Grim. Then Thorstein became very weary, so that he was hardly able to stand. He saw that he would fall; and of the opposite party all had fallen but Gautan and Ogautan. Now Thorer was both weary and wounded, and the night was already growing very dark. Just then Thorstein turned against Gautan and stabbed him through his body with Angervadil, so that he fell to the ground among the other dead bodies. Then three men, Jokul, Grim, and Ogautan, arose and searched for Thorstein among the slain, and they thought they had found him, but the person they found was Jokul's brother, Finn, for they were so much like each other that it was impossible to know them apart. Grim said Thorstein was dead. Said Ogautan: 'That shall be put beyond a doubt, and he cut his head off, but of course it did not bleed, for he was already dead. After this they went home. King Njorfe asked them how the meeting had turned out, and learning this, he did not approve it at all, saying that he now had lost much more than his son Olaf, his seven sons and many other men having died. Now Jokul kept quiet.

XIII

IN the next place it is to be told that Thorstein lay among the slain so tired out that he was wholly unable to help himself, but

he was but little wounded. And toward the end of the night he heard a wagon coming along the ice. Then he saw a man following the wagon, and he saw that the man was his father. And when the man came to the field of battle, he cleared his way, throwing the dead out of his path, but he threw none with more force than the sons of the king. He saw that all were dead except Thorstein and Thorer. He then asked them whether they could speak at all, and Thorer said that he could. Still Viking saw that he was covered with gaping wounds. Thorstein said that he was not wounded, but very tired. Viking took Thorer in his lap, and then it seemed to Thorstein that his father, in spite of his age, showed great strength. Thorstein went to the wagon himself and laid himself in it with his weapons. Then Viking drove on with the wagon. The weather began to grow dark and cloudy, and it changed so fast that, in a very little while, the whole ice seemed to Viking to give way. Just at the time when they had landed, all the ice had melted out of the lake. Then Viking went home to his bed-chamber. Close by his bed was the entrance to an underground dwelling, and down into it, he took his sons; in it was enough of food and drink, and clothing, and all things that might be needed. Viking healed the wounds of his son Thorer, for he was a good leech. One end of the house stood in a forest; and here Viking very strongly warned his sons never to leave the underground dwelling, for he said it was sure that Ogautan would straightway find out that they were alive; and then, added he, we may soon look for a war. As to this they made good promises. Time passed on until Thorer became altogether whole again. It was now talked abroad throughout the country that all the sons of Viking were dead; but nevertheless, it was talked somewhat after Ogautan that it was not sure whether Thorer was dead or not. Then Jokul bade him seek and try to find out with certainty where Thorer had his dwelling-place. Now Ogautan fell into deep thinking, but still he did not become any surer about Thorer. One day it happened that Thorer said to Thorstein: 'I am getting very tired of staying in this underground dwelling, now the weather is fine, and my will is that we take a walk into the forest to amuse ourselves.' Answered Thorstein: 'I will not, for we would then break the bidding of our father.' 'Nevertheless, I shall go,' said Thorer. Thorstein had no mind to stay behind, and so they went to the forest and spent the day there amusing themselves. But in the evening, when they were about to go home again, they saw a little she-fox scenting round about her in all directions, and snuffing under every tree. Said Thorer: 'What Satanic being goes there, brother?' Answered Thorstein: 'I really do not know; it seems to me that I have once seen something like it, namely, the night before Jokul's visit to the shed, and I think that we here have the cursed Ogautan.' He then took a spear, which he shot at the fox, but she crept down into the ground. After this they went home to their underground dwelling, and did not let on that anything had happened. Shortly afterward, jarl Viking came there and said: 'Now you have done a bad thing, having broken what I bade you, by leaving the cave, and thus Ogautan has found out that you are here. I therefore expect the brothers soon will come with war upon us.'

XIV

SHORTLY after this, Ogautan had a talk with Jokul and said: 'It is indeed true that I am your right and not your left hand.' 'What is there now about that?' asked Jokul. Answered Ogautan: 'It is that the brothers, Thorer and Thorstein, are still alive at Viking's, and are hid by him.' Answered Jokul: 'Then I will gather together men, and not give up till we have their lives.' Jokul got together eighty men, among whom there were thirty of the king's courtiers, all well dressed. In the evening they prepared for setting out, being about to leave the next morning. Two young loafers, of whom the one was called Vott and the other Thumal, had just come there, and when they had just gone to bed in the evening, Vott spoke to Thumal: 'Do you not think it is wise, brother, that we arise and go to Viking, and tell him of Jokul's plans, for I know it will be the bane of Viking if they come upon him unawares, and it is our duty to go and help him.' Made answer Thumal: 'You are very foolish; do you not think that the watchmen will become aware of us if we travel by night, and then we shall be killed without giving any help to Viking.' Said Vott: 'You always show that you are a coward; but although you dare not move a step, I will nevertheless go and tell Viking what is about being done, for I would gladly lose my life if I could hinder the death of Viking and his sons, for he has often been kind to me.' Then Vott arose and dressed himself, and likewise did also Thumal, for the latter had now no mind of staying in the bed alone. Now they went their way, and came to Viking's at midnight, and aroused him from his sleep. Vott told him that Jokul was to be looked for there with a large number of men. Said Viking: 'Well have you done, dear Vott, and your deed surely deserves a reward.' Then Viking called together some men from the neighbourhood, so that he had thirty men. Then he went down to his sons in the cave, and told them the state of things. Said Thorer: 'They shall be withstood if they come, for we will come up out of the cave and fight together with you.' Answered Viking: 'You shall not! Let us first see how our fight may turn out, and if it should look hopeless to me, then I will go to that place below which is your cave and make a great noise, and then you must come and help me.' Thorstein said he would do so, and so Viking went away. After daybreak Viking and all his men took their weapons. He took the kesia called Harek's loom in his hand; but everybody thought he would not be able to wield it on account of its weight, he being so old. A wonderful change then seemed to take place; for as soon as Viking had put on the armour he seemed to be young a second time. A large yard was inclosed by a high wall in front of Viking's byre; it formed a very good vantage ground, and here he and his men prepared themselves for the battle, and weapons were given to Vott and Thumal.

XV

NOW it is to be told that Jokul busked himself and all his army for starting early the next morning, and he did not halt in his march before he came to the dwellings of Viking. Viking was standing outside upon the wall of the yard, and bade Jokul and all his men come in. Answered Jokul: 'Quite otherwise have you deserved

than that we should accept your invitation; our errand here is that you give up those mishap-bringing men, Thorstein and Thorer.' 'I will not do it,' answered Viking; 'nevertheless I will not deny that both of them have been here, but I would sooner give up myself than them. Now you may attack us if you like, but I and my men will ward ourselves.' They now made a hard attack, but Viking and his men warded themselves bravely. Thus some time passed. Then Jokul tried to scale the wall. Viking and his men slew many men; but now all his own men began to fall. Then Viking went to the place over the underground dwelling, struck his shield hard, and made a fearful noise. This Thorer heard, and said to Thorstein: 'We ought to make haste, and for all that we may be too late, for I think our father has fallen already.' Thorstein said he was quite ready, and when they came out only Vott and Thumal and three other men were standing with Viking. Nevertheless Viking was not wounded yet; he was only very tired. As soon as the brothers came out, Thorstein turned to the spot where Jokul was standing, but Thorer went where Ogautan and his men stood. Twelve of king Njorfe's men attacked Viking and his men. Viking warded himself, and was not wounded by the men who were against him. Their leader was called Bjorn. In a short time Thorer slew all the followers of Ogautan, and stabbed at him with his sword, but Ogautan thrust himself down into the ground, so that only the soles of his feet could be seen. Thorstein attacked Jokul. Said Vott: 'It is well that you are trying each other's bravery, for Jokul never could bear to hear that Thorstein was a match for him in anything.' Now there was a very hard battle between Thorstein and Jokul, and it so turned out that Jokul, scarred with many wounds, bounded back, and fell down outside of the wall. But when Jokul had gone away, Viking gave quarter to the men of the king's court that still were alive, and sent them away with suitable gifts, begging them to bring his friendly greetings to king Njorfe. And when Jokul came home, Ogautan was there already. Jokul blamed him bitterly for having fled before anybody else. To this made answer Ogautan: 'It was not possible to stay in the fight any longer, and truly it may be said that we there had to do with trolls rather than with men.' But Jokul found that his words rather overdid the matter. Somewhat later king Njorfe's men, to whom quarter had been given by Viking and his men, came home, bringing Viking's greetings to king Njorfe, and telling him of all the kind treatment they had gotten from Viking. Said the king: 'Truly is Viking unlike most other men, on account of his high-mindedness and all his bravery, and now, my son Jokul, I speak the truth when I solemnly forbid any war to be waged against Viking from this time forward.' Answered Jokul: 'I cannot bear to have the slayers of my brothers in the garth next to me, and in a word, I declare that Viking and his sons shall never live in peace so far as I am concerned, and I shall never cease persecuting them before they are all sent to Hel (the goddess of death).' Answered the king: 'Then I shall try and see who of us two is the more blest with friends, for with all those who are willing to follow me I will go and help Viking; it seems to me to be of great weight that you do not become the bane of Viking, for if that should follow, I would be forced to do one of two things, either to have you killed, and that would be the cause of evil talk, or to break my oaths which I have sworn, namely, that I would avenge Viking if I should outlive

him.' And thus he ended his speech. Viking had a talk with his sons, and said to them: 'Owing to Jokul's power I dare not keep you here; but there is another matter of still more weight, and that is, that I do not want any discord to arise between me and king Njorfe.' Said Thorstein: 'What will you then advise us to do?' Answered Viking: 'There is a man, by name Halfdan, who rules over Vags; Vags is on the other side of yonder mountain. Halfdan is my old friend and foster-brother. To him I will send you, and commend you to his good will; but there are many dangerous hindrances in the way, especially two hut-dwellers (robbers), one of whom is worse to deal with than the other; the name of one of them is Sam, and the other is called Fullafle; the latter has a dog called Gram, with which it is almost as dangerous to deal as with the robber himself. Now I am not sure that you will reach Vags, though you may escape both of these robbers, for there is a chasm along the mountain so deep and broad that I do not know any one who has passed it but my foster-brothers and myself; but I should indeed think it more likely that Thorstein might pass it, whereas I feel less hopeful about Thorer.' Shortly afterward the brothers busked themselves for setting out, having all their weapons with them. Then Viking gave the kesia to Thorer; he handed a gold ring to his son Thorstein, begging him to give it to Halfdan as a token of their old friendship.

'Now be patient my son Thorer,' said Viking; 'although Halfdan may be peevish toward you, or does not look much to you or your errand.' Then the sons took leave of their father, who was so deeply moved that the tears trickled down his cheeks. Viking looked after them as they were going away, and said: 'I shall never in my life see you again, and nevertheless you, my son Thorstein, will reach an old age, and become a very distinguished man; and now farewell, and all hail to you both.' Then the old man returned home, but his sons climbed the mountain until they reached a hut in the evening. The door was half shut. Thorer stepped over to it, and by using all his strength, he pushed it open; and when they had entered the hut, they saw there a great deal of wares and supplies of all kinds. There was a large bed. And at nightfall the hut-dweller, a man of somewhat frowning look, came home. He said: 'Are you here, you mishap-bringing men – you sons of Viking, Thorstein and Thorer, who have slain seven of the sons of Njorfe? And now all their ill-luck shall come to an end, for it will be an easy matter for me to strike you to the ground.' 'Who is that,' said Thorer, 'who so boastingly insults us?' Answered the robber: 'My name is Sam; I am the son of Svart; my brother's name is Fullafle; he is boss in the other hut.' Said Thorstein: 'I see that feyness[2] calls on us two brothers, if you alone kill both of us, and therefore I do not hesitate to test our valour, but Thorer shall stand by without taking any part in our combat.' At the same time Sam ran suddenly under Thorstein with so great speed, that the latter lost the hold he had gotten, but still did not fall. Then Thorer ran to Sam, stabbing him with his kesia in one side so that it came out at the other side, and thus Sam fell down dead. So they stopped there during the night and had a good rest, for there was plenty of food. They made the hut warm, but did not carry away any fee with them. In the morning they left the hut,

[2] Feyness (Icel. feig'S) means the approach or foreboding of death.

but in the evening of the same day they came to another hut, much larger than the former one. There also the door was half shut. Thorer stepped over to the door, intending to push it open, but he could not. He used all his strength, but still the door would not open. Then Thorstein stepped over to the door, and pushed it until it gave way, and so they went into the hut. On the one side there was a stack of wares and on the other one of logs; a bed was placed in the inner part of the hut, crosswise, and it was so large that they were surprised at its size. At one end of the bed was something like a large, round bedstead, and they judged that it must be the couch of the dog Gram. They then seated themselves and built a fire before them, and long after nightfall they heard heavy footsteps outside; presently the door was opened, and a giant of stupendous stature entered, carrying bound on his back a large bear, and a string of fowl on his breast. He laid his burden down on the floor, saying: 'Fie! here I have the miscreants, the sons of Viking, who, on account of their ill-fated deeds, are held in the worst repute throughout the whole land. But how did you escape the hands of my brother Sam?' 'We escaped in such a manner,' said Thorstein, 'that he lay dead on the spot.' 'You have taken advantage of him in his sleep,' said Fullafle. 'By no means,' said Thorstein, 'for we fought with him, and my brother Thorer slew him.' 'I shall not act as a nithing toward you tonight,' said Fullafle; 'you shall stay till tomorrow morning, and have what food you want.' Then the hut-dweller cut his game to pieces, took a table and put victuals on it, whereupon they all took to eating, and after their supper they went to bed. The two brothers slept together in some marketable cloaks. The dog growled as they passed by him. Neither party tried to deceive the other. In the morning both parties arose early. Said Fullafle: 'Now, Thorstein, let us try each other's strength, but let Thorer fight with my dog in another place.' Answered Thorstein: 'That shall be according to your wish.' Now they went out of the hut and over on the lawn which fronted it, and suddenly the dog, with his jaws wide open, leaped upon Thorer. Both Thorer and the dog fought fiercely, for the dog warded off every blow with his tail, and when Thorer tried to pierce him with his kesia, he escaped by biting the weapon at every stab. Thus they fought for three hours, and Thorer had not yet succeeded in wounding him. Once Gram suddenly darted upon Thorer and bit a slice out of his calf. At the same time Thorer stabbed the dog with his kesia, pinning him down to the ground, and soon after Gram expired. But of Fullafle it is to be told that he had a large meker (Anglo-Saxon mece, a kind of sword) in his hand, and Thorstein had his sword also. They had a long and severe struggle; for Fullafle was wont to deal heavy blows, but as Angervadil bit armour no less than flesh, he fell dead, and Thorstein was wholly without a wound.

XVI

NOW the brothers busked themselves for leaving, and continued their walk until they reached a great chasm, which it seemed to Thorstein it would be very dangerous to pass. Nevertheless, he made himself ready to leap over the abyss, and did it. He was immediately followed by Thorer, but when Thorstein had reached

the other side of the chasm and looked round, Thorer had just reached the same side and was falling down into the chasm. Thorstein succeeded, however, in seizing him and pulling him up again. Said Thorstein then: 'Brother, you always show that you are a dauntless fellow; so you did now, too, for you might know that it would be certain death to you if you should fall into the chasm.' 'It did not happen this time,' answered Thorer, 'for you saved me, as you have so often done before.' Then they proceeded on their journey until they came to a large river, which was both deep and rapid. Thorstein said they must look for the ford, but without delay Thorer waded into the river, and not far from the bank the water was so deep that the bottom could not be reached, and therefore he had to sustain himself by swimming. Thorstein not being minded to be standing on the bank, threw himself into the river and swam after him. Thus they reached the other bank, where they wrung their wet clothes. But while they were doing this the weather grew so bitterly cold that their clothes froze hard as a stone, and so they could not put them on. At the same time a fearful snow storm arose, and it was thought that Ogautan was the cause of it. Thorstein asked Thorer what was the best thing for them to do. Answered Thorer: 'I think we can do nothing better than to dip our clothes in the river, for in cold water things soon thaw out.' So they did, and thereby were able to put on their clothes again. Then they went on until they came to the byre of Vags. It being night when they came there, the door of the house was locked, so they could not enter. They kept knocking at the door a long time, but nobody came to it. In the yard lay a beam twenty fathoms long. This they brought upon the roofs of the

houses, and they rode upon it in such a manner that every timber began to creak, and all the inmates of the house became so frightened that they ran each into his corner. Then Halfdan went to the door and out to the front yard, and the brothers now went over to him and greeted him. Halfdan gave them a cold and reserved answer, asking them, however, for their names. They gave him their names, adding that they were the sons of jarl Viking, and that they brought greetings from the latter to him. Said Halfdan: 'I cannot talk about foster-brothership between us; to me it seems that many a man keeps his word of foster-brothership but middlingly well, and no more; and as for you, who have slain the most of king Njorfe's sons, it also seems to me that you have not regarded the sanctity of foster-brothership in respect to many of Njorfe's descendants. Still, you may enter my house, and lodge here tonight, if you like.' Then Halfdan went in at a swinging pace, followed by the brothers. They entered the stofa (sitting-room), where there were but few persons. Nobody took the clothes off the brothers, and thus they sat during the evening, till people began to go to bed; then a dish, containing porridge, and a spoon in each end of it, was placed on the table before them. Thorer began to eat the porridge. Said Thorstein then: 'You are very inconsistent in regard to your pride'; and, so saying, he took the dish and threw it on the floor in the further part of the room, so that it broke to pieces. Hereupon the people went to bed. The brothers had no bed, and got but very little sleep during the night. Early in the morning they got up and busked themselves for leaving. But when they had got outside the door the old man came to them and asked them: 'What did you say last night, or whose

sons did you say you were?' Made answer Thorer: 'What more do you know now than when we told you we were the sons of jarl Viking?' Said Thorstein: 'Here is a golden finger-ring, which he begged me to give you.' Said Thorer: 'I think he will be the worse off who shows him anything of it.' Made answer Thorstein: 'Be not so peevish, brother! Here is the gold ring, as a token that you should receive us in such a manner that we might be comforted and protected at your house.' Halfdan took the ring, became glad, and said: 'Why should I not receive you, and do all the good in my power for you? To do so is my duty, on account of my relations to my friend Viking. You seem to be men blest with good luck.' Said Thorer: 'The adage is indeed a true one, that it is good to have two mouths for the two kinds of speech. Last night, soon after we had come to you, you treated us quite otherwise. I therefore am inclined to think you a coward, and you everywhere show your slyness.' Said Thorstein: 'Let us be patient, Halfdan, with my brother, although he is cross in his words to you, for he is a reckless man in his words and doings.' Answered Halfdan: 'I have heard that you are the most doughty of men, and that Thorer is hot-tempered and reckless; still, I think that you are in every respect a man of more spirit.' Hereupon they went into the house, their clothes were taken off them, and every attention was shown them. They stayed there during the winter, and enjoyed the most hearty treatment. But in the beginning of spring Thorstein said to Halfdan: 'We shall now leave this place.' Answered Halfdan: 'What is your best advice?' Made answer Thorstein: 'I wish you would give me a ship, manned with a crew, for I intend to set out and wage war and gain booty.' To this Halfdan gave his consent. After busking themselves properly, they sailed to the south, along the coast of the country, until they met with two vessels, which had been sent out by their father, and were filled with men and good weapons. Now Thorstein sent back the ship which had been given to him by Halfdan, and sent the crew with it; but the brothers became skippers, one on each of the two ships. They waged wars in many places during the summer, and gained much fee and fame. In the autumn they landed on an island which was ruled by the bonde, whose name was Grim. He bade them stay with him through the winter, and they accepted his offer. Grim was married and had an only daughter, by name Thora, a tall and fine-looking girl. Thorer fell in love with her, and told his brother Thorstein that he wanted to marry her. Thorstein talked about the matter to Grim, the bonde, but the latter flatly refused to give his consent. Answered Thorstein: 'Then I challenge you to fight with me in a holm-gang, and he who wins shall be master of your daughter.' Grim said he was ready for the holm-gang. The next day they took a blanket, which they threw under their feet, and then they fought the whole day very bravely, but in the evening they parted, neither of them having received any wound. The second and the third days they fought, but the results were the same as the first day. One day Thorer asked the daughter of the bonde how it came to pass that Grim could not be vanquished. She said there was in the fore part of his helmet a stone, which made him quite invincible as long as it was not taken away from him. This Thorer told to Thorstein; and on the fourth day of their fight Thorstein threw his sword, grasping the helmet of his antagonist with both his hands with so great force that the cords of the helmet were

severed. Shortly after he attacked Grim, and now Thorstein's greater strength was shown. He brought Grim down, but gave him quarter. Then Grim asked who had advised him to take the helmet. Thorstein said that Thora had told it to Thorer. 'Then she wants to be married,' answered Grim, 'and it shall so be.' Thus it was resolved that Thorer should marry Thora. In the beginning of spring Thorstein set out to carry on wars, leaving Thorer at home. The newly married couple took to loving each other very much, and they got a son, whom they named Harald. This was their only child. He afterward took his father's kesia, after which he was nick-named and was called Harald Kesia.

XVII

A KING was named Skate, a son of Erik, who again was a son of Myndil Meitalfsson. Skate was king in Sogn, and with his queen he had two children, a son named Bele, who was a very excellent man, and a daughter named Ingeborg. At this time she was not in the kingdom, having been spellbound (and thus removed from the country). Skate had been a berserk and a very great viking, and he had forced his way onto the throne of Sogn. There was a man named Thorgrim, who had to defend the realm against the invasion of foes. He was a great champion and a warlike man, but not over faithful. Between Thorgrim and the king's son, Bele, there was a warm friendship. Bele had great celebrity throughout all lands. It had happened, after king Skate had grown very old, both his children still being young, that two vikings,

one named Gautan and the other Ogautan, had landed in his country. They had taken the king by surprise, and offered him two conditions, either to fight a battle with them, or give up his land and become a jarl under them. King Skate, though he had no troops to meet them with, would rather die with honour than live with shame; he would rather fall in his kingdom than serve his foes. He therefore went to battle, having no other troops than his courtiers. Thorgrim escaped with the king's son, Bele, but Ingeborg remained at home in her bower. In the combat with Ogautan, king Skate fell with honour, but those of his men who escaped death in the battle fled to the woods. Now Ogautan took the kingdom into his charge, and had the title of king given to himself. He asked Ingeborg to become his wife, but she flatly refused, saying she would rather kill herself than marry the bane of her father, and such a villain, too, as Ogautan; for you, she said, are more like the devil himself than like a man. At this Ogautan grew angry, and said: 'I shall reward you for your foul language, and I hereby enchant you, so that you shall get the same stature and looks as my sister Skellinefja, and the same nature also as she, as far as you may be capable of assuming it; and, spell-bound, you shall inhabit that cave which is on the Deep River, and you shall never escape out of this enchanted state until some man of noble birth is willing to have you, and pledges himself to marry you; still you can never escape until I am dead. But my sister shall wear your looks.' Said Ingeborg: 'I cause you to be so enchanted that you shall keep this kingdom only for a short time, and never have any good of your reign.' The spells pronounced by Ogautan proved true, and Ingeborg disappeared. Soon afterward, the king's

son, Bele, came thither again, together with Thorgrim and many other men. It was night, and they set fire to the upper story of the house in which the two brothers slept, and burnt it up, together with the people who lived in it, except the brothers, who escaped through an underground passage and fled, without stopping until they came to the court of king Njorfe. Bele took possession of his country again, and Thorgrim remained in his former position as warder of the king's land.

XVIII

A KING, named Vilhjalm (William), ruled over Valland. He was a wise man, and was blest with many friends. He had a daughter, who was named Olof, and was a woman of great culture. Now it is to be told that Jokul, Njorfe's son, after the departure of the sons of Viking, made Thorstein and Thorer outlaws in every place within the boundaries of his kingdom. King Njorfe did not consent to it, for he and Viking kept their friendship during their whole life. Once Ogautan had a talk with Jokul, and asked him if he would not like to get married. Jokul asked him where he saw a match for him. Answered Ogautan: 'Vilhjalm of Valland has a daughter named Olof, and I think a marriage with her would add to your honour.' Said Jokul: 'Why not then make up our minds as to this subject?' So they busked themselves for the voyage, and together with sixty men they sailed for Valland. Here they paid a visit to king Vilhjalm, who received Jokul very heartily, for his father, Njorfe, was well known throughout all lands. Now

Jokul asked for Olof in marriage, and Ogautan pleaded with the king in his behalf, but the latter appealed to his daughter. And straightway after this conversation thirty very brave-looking men entered the hall. The one who went before them was the tallest and fairest, and he went up to the king and greeted him. As soon as Ogautan saw these men his voice fell, his beard sunk, and he begged Jokul and his other men not to mention his name so long as they stayed in that land. The king asked the stately men their names, and the chief called himself Bele, and said he was the son of Skate, the king, who was ruler of Sogn. 'My errand hither,' he added, 'is to woo your daughter.' Made answer the king: 'Jokul, the son of Njorfe, came here before you on the same errand; now I will settle the matter in this way, that she choose herself which one of the two wooers she will have.' Then the king placed Bele on one side of himself, and there was a great banquet. After three nights they took a walk to the bower of the princess, asking her which one of the two wooers, Jokul or Bele, she would marry, and it soon appeared that she would rather marry Bele; but at that moment Ogautan threw a round piece of wood into her lap, whereby her nature was suddenly changed to such an extent that she refused Bele and married Jokul. Then Bele returned to his ships. Jokul and Bele had formerly been on good terms, so that some people say that Bele had got a reward for killing Thorstein and Thorer. Bele did not blame Jokul though the daughter of the king declined to marry him (Bele), for the matter depended upon her decision. Thereupon Bele went home to his kingdom, and after the wedding Jokul also repaired homeward accompanied by Ogautan.

XIX

NOW our saga must turn to Thorstein at the time when he was returning home from his warfare, bound for Grim the bonde, for his brother Thorer resided in that island. Jokul got news of Thorstein's voyages. He spoke to Ogautan, asking him to try his tricks and by witchcraft bring about a storm against Thorstein, in order that he might be drowned, together with all his men. Ogautan said he would try, no matter what the result might be. Then, with his incantations, he caused so tremendous a storm against Thorstein that his ships were wrecked amid the tumultuous waves, and all his crew perished. Thorstein held out well a long time, but at last he became tired of swimming, and then he had reached the surf and was beginning to sink down. At this moment he saw an old woman, of very great stature, wading from the shore out toward him. She wore a shrivelled skin-cloak, which fell to her feet in front, but was very short behind, and her face was very large and like that of a monster. She stepped over to him and, seizing him up from the sea, said: 'Will you accept life from me, Thorstein?' Answered he: 'Why should I not, or what is your name?' Said she: 'My name is uncommon; it is Skellinefja; but you will have to make some sacrifice in return for your life.' Said he: 'What is it?' Made answer she: 'That you grant me the favour that I ask of you.' Said Thorstein: 'You will ask nothing from me that will not bring me good luck; but when shall the favour be granted?' Answered she: 'Not yet.' Then she bore him ashore, and now he had come to that island which was governed by Grim. She then wrestled with him till he grew warm, whereupon they parted, each wishing the other success. Then she walked on, for she said she had other places to call at. But Thorstein went home to the byre, and his meeting there with his brother was the cause of great joy to both of them; and so Thorstein remained there during the winter, and very much was made of him. Now we must turn to Jokul and Ogautan as they were sailing homeward. One very fine day it happened that their ship was suddenly shrouded in darkness, accompanied by such a biting frost and cold that nobody on board dared to turn his face against the wind. They all covered their faces with their clothes; but when the weather had cleared off again they saw Ogautan hanging in the hole of the mast-head, and he was dead. Jokul looked upon his death as a great loss, and returning to his kingdom he remained quiet. Early the next spring Thorstein and Thorer busked themselves for a voyage, intending to visit their father, Viking; and when they came as far as to Deep River, before they knew of it, Jokul came there to them with thirty men. A combat between them straightway began. Jokul was very eager in the fight, and so was his brother Grim. Thorer and Thorstein defended themselves bravely, and a long time passed before these brothers received any wounds from Jokul and his men, for not only did Thorstein deal heavy blows, but Angervadil also bit iron as well as cloth. Thorer defended himself excellently, although he did not have his kesia, which he had left at home. He and Grim met, and they fought very bravely; still the end of the fight was that Grim fell to the ground, dead. By this time Thorstein had slain eighteen men, but, as might be expected, he was both tired and wounded, and so was Thorer. Then the brothers turned their backs together and still defended

themselves well. Now Jokul, with his eleven men, pursued them and made so valiant an attack that Thorer fell. Then Thorstein defended himself manfully until there remained no more than Jokul and three of his men. But then Jokul stabbed Thorstein with his sword, wounding him in the upper part of the thigh; and Jokul being a strong man, and bearing on the sword with all his might while he stabbed him, Thorstein, who was very tired, and was standing on the very edge of the riverbank, fell down from the crag, while it was all that Jokul could do to stop himself so that he did not fall also. After this Jokul went home, thinking he had slain Thorstein and Thorer; and having come home he remained quiet. But now it is to be told of Thorstein, that he, having fallen from the crag, alighted upon a grassy spot among the rocks; but, being tired and wounded, he was unable to move, and yet he was in his full senses after he had fallen. Angervadil fell out of his hand and down into the river. Thorstein was lying there betwixt life and death, and expecting soon to breathe his last. But before he had lain thus very long he saw Skellinefja coming; she was clad in her skin-gown, and looked no fairer than before. She approached the place where Thorstein was lying, and said: 'It seems to me, Thorstein, that your misfortunes will never come to an end, and now you seem already to be breathing your last, or will you now grant me the favour upon which we formerly agreed?' Said Thorstein: 'I do not now find myself able to render much of any service to you.' Made answer she: 'My request is that you promise to marry me, and then I will try to heal your wounds.' Said Thorstein: 'I do not know as I had better make that promise, for to me you look like a monster.' Said she: 'Still you have your choice between these two things. You must either marry me or lose your life; and, in the latter case, you break, in the bargain, the oath which you swore to me when you pledged yourself to grant my favour after I had saved you at Grim's Island.' Said Thorstein: 'There is much truth in your words, and it is better to keep one's promise; hence I vow that I will marry you, and you will prove to be my best helper in time of need; still I should like to stipulate with you that you get me my sword back, so that I may wear it in case my life is prolonged.' Said she: 'So be it.' And having taken him up in her skin-gown, she leaped, as if quite unencumbered, up over the crags and proceeded until a large cave was before them. Having entered the cave, she bandaged Thorstein's wounds and laid him on a soft bed, and within seven nights he was almost healed. One day Skellinefja had left the cave, and in the evening she came back with the sword, which was then dripping wet, and she gave it to Thorstein. Said she: 'Now I have saved your life twice and given you your sword back, of which you are fonder than of aught else; and a fourth thing, which is of great importance to both of us, is that I hanged Ogautan. And yet you have completely rewarded me, for you have delivered me from the spell-bound condition into which Ogautan enchanted me. My name is Ingeborg; I am the daughter of king Skate and the sister of Bele, but my only means of delivery from bondage was that some man of noble birth should promise to marry me. Now you have done this, and I am freed from bondage. Now you must busk yourself for leaving the cave and follow my advices, and you will find my brother Bele and four men with him. Among the latter will be his land-warden, Thorgrim Kobbe. From Jokul

they have received some money, offered as a price for your head, and they will begin a battle with you. I do not care if you do kill Thorgrim and his companions, but spare the life of my brother Bele, for I should like to have you become his foster-brother; and if you have a mind to marry me, then go with him home to Sogn and woo me. I shall be there before you, and it may be that I will look otherwise to you then than now.' Then they parted, and he had not gone far before he met Bele, accompanied by four men, and, at their meeting, Thorgrim said: 'It is good, Thorstein, that we have found each other. Now we shall try to win the price put upon your head by Jokul.' Said Thorstein: 'It seems possible to me that you may lose the fee and forfeit your life too.'

XX

NOW we must tell about Thorstein that he was attacked by Bele and his men, but he defended himself well and bravely, and the result was that Thorgrim and three of his companions fell. Then Thorstein and Bele entered a new contest. Thorstein defended himself, but would not wound Bele. Bele kept on attacking Thorstein, until the latter seized him and set him down at his side, saying: 'You are wholly in my power, but I will not only give you your life, but also offer you an opportunity to become my foster-brother. You shall be king and I shall be herser, and in addition to this I will woo your sister Ingeborg, and get her estates in Sogn as a dowry.' Said Bele: 'This is no very easy matter, for my sister has disappeared, so that nobody knows what has become of her.' Answered Thorstein: 'She may have come back.' Said Bele: 'I do not see how she could get a doughtier fellow than you are, and I give my full consent to the proposition.' Having settled this with their words of honour, they went home to Sogn. Bele soon became aware that his sister had come back, and that she had not lost any of that blooming beauty which she had had before in her youthful days. Thorstein began his suit, and asked that Ingeborg might become his wife. This was resolved upon. As a dowry she got from her home all the possessions lying on the other side of the fjord. The byre where Thorstein resided was called Framness, but the byre governed by Bele was called Syrstrond. The next spring Thorstein and Bele set out to wage wars, having five ships, and during the summer they harried far and wide, and got enough of booty, but in the autumn they returned home again having seven ships. The next summer they went out a harrying again, but got very little booty, for all vikings shunned them; and having reached the small rocky islands called Elfarsker, they anchored in a harbour in the evening. Thorstein and Bele went ashore, and crossed that ness (peninsula) toward which their ships were lying. But having crossed the ness, they saw twelve ships covered with black tilts. On shore they saw tents, from which smoke arose, and they seemed to be sure that these tents must be occupied by cooks. Having taken on a disguise, they went thither, and having come to the door of a tent, they both placed themselves in it in such a manner that the smoke did not find any out-way. The cooks made use of abusive words, and asked what sort of beggars they were, as they were guileful enough to want them burnt alive or smothered. Bele and Thorstein made an ugly disturbance, and

answered with hoarse voices that they came to get food; or, said they, who is the excellent man who commands the fleet lying here at the shore? Said they: 'You must be stupid old men if you have not heard of Ufe, who is called Ufe the Unlucky, and is the son of Herbrand the Bigheaded. This Ufe is the brother of Otunfaxe, and we know there are no men under the sun more celebrated than these two brothers.' Said Thorstein: 'You tell good tidings.' Shortly after, Thorstein and Bele returned to their own men, and early the next morning, having busked themselves, they rowed around the ness and immediately shouted the cry of battle. The others then quickly busked themselves, took their weapons, and a vehement battle began. Ufe had more men, and was himself a most valiant warrior. They fought for a long time in such a manner that it could not be seen which side would gain the victory. But on the third day Thorstein began to board the dragon commanded by Ufe the Unlucky, and he was followed without delay by Bele, and a great havoc they made, killing all who were between the prow and the mast of the ship. Then Ufe came from the poop and attacked Bele, and they fought for some time, until Bele began to get wounds from Ufe, who handled his weapon dexterously and dealt heavy blows. Meanwhile Thorstein came with his Angervadil, and gave Ufe a blow with it. The sword hit the helmet, split the whole body and the byrnie-clad man from head to foot, and Angervadil struck against the mast-beam so forcibly that both its edges sunk out of sight. Said Bele: 'This blow of yours, foster-brother, will live in the memory of men as long as the North is peopled.' Hereupon they offered to the vikings two terms, either to give up and save their lives, or to have a combat. But they preferred to accept a quarter from Thorstein and Bele. The latter gave pardon to all, and they eagerly accepted it. Here much booty was taken, and having stayed three nights, during which time the wounded were healed, they repaired home in the autumn.

XXI

AT springtime the foster-brothers busked themselves for leaving home, and had fifteen ships. Bele commanded the dragon which had been owned by Ufe the Unlucky. It was a choice ship, its beak and stern being whittled and carved and extensively overlaid with gold. King Bele got the dragon, for it was the choicest part of the booty which they took when they had slain Ufe, it always being their custom to give to Bele the most costly parts of the booty. No ship was thought better than this dragon excepting Ellide, which was owned by Ufe's brother, Otunfaxe. Ufe and Otunfaxe had inherited these ships from their father, Herbrand, and Ellide was the better one of the two in these respects, that it had fair wind wherever it sailed, and it almost understood human speech. But the reason why Otunfaxe and not Ufe had gotten Ellide was, that Ufe had fallen into so bad luck that he had killed both his father and his mother, and it seemed to Otunfaxe that if justice should be done, Ufe had forfeited his right of inheritance. Otunfaxe was the superior of the two brothers on account of his strength, stature and witchcraft. Now the foster-brothers went out a harrying, and waged wars far and wide in the waters of the Baltic, but they found but very few vikings, for everybody, upon hearing of them,

fled out of their reach. At this time none were more celebrated for their harrying exploits than Thorstein and Bele. One day the foster-brothers were standing on a promontory, on the other side of which they saw twelve ships lying at anchor, and all of them were very large. They rowed rapidly toward the ships and asked who was the commander of the warriors. A man who stood leaning against the mast made answer: 'Angantyr is my name; I am a son of jarl Hermund of Gautland.' Said Thorstein: 'You are a hopeful fellow; but how old are you?' Made answer he: 'I am now nineteen years old.' Asked Bele: 'Which do you prefer, to give up your ships and fee or to fight a battle with us?' Said Angantyr: 'The more unequal your terms are, the more promptly I make my choice. I prefer to defend my fee, and fall, sword in hand, if such be my fate.' Said Bele: 'Busk yourself then; but we will make the attack.' Then both of them busked themselves for the battle and took their weapons. Said Thorstein to Bele: 'There is very little of noble courage in attacking them with fifteen ships, as they have but twelve.' Said Bele: 'Why shall we not lay three of our ships aside?' And so they did. A hard battle was now fought. Angantyr's warriors dealt so heavy blows, that Bele and Thorstein declared that they had never been in greater peril. They fought the whole day until evening, but in such a manner that it could not be seen which party would gain the victory. The next day they busked themselves again for the fight. Then said Angantyr: 'To me it seems, king Bele, that it would be wiser not to sacrifice any more of our men, but let us two fight a duel, and he who conquers the other in the holm-gang shall be the victorious party.' Bele accepted this challenge; so they went ashore, and having thrown a blanket under their feet, they fought bravely until Bele became tired out and began to receive wounds. Thorstein thought it evident that Bele would not gain the victory over Angantyr, and it came to pass that Bele was not only exhausted but also nigh his last breath. Said Thorstein then: 'It seems best to me, Angantyr, that you cease your fighting, for I see that Bele is so exhausted that he is almost gone. On the other hand, I will not be mean enough to play the dastard toward you and assist him; but if you become the bane of Bele, then I will challenge you to fight a duel with me; and as to personal valour and strength, I think there is no less difference between me and you than there is between you and Bele. I will slay you in a holm-gang duel, and it would be a great loss if you both die. Now I offer you this condition, that if you spare Bele's life, we will enter into a foster-brotherhood upon mutual oaths.' Said Angantyr: 'To me it seems a fair offer that Bele and I enter into foster-brotherhood; but it seems to me a great favour that I may become your foster-brother.' Then this was resolved upon and secured by firm pledges on both sides. They opened a vein in the hollow of their hands, crept beneath the sod,[3] and there they solemnly swore that each of them should avenge the other if any one of them should be slain by weapons. Then they reviewed their warriors, and two ships of each party had lost all their men. They healed those who were wounded, and thereupon they left the place with twenty-three ships, returning home in the autumn. They spent the winter at home quietly, and

[3] There was a heathen rite of creeping under a sod partially detached from the earth, and letting the blood mix with the mould. Persons forming a foster-brotherhood would make use of this ceremony.

enjoyed great honour. Now none were thought more famous on account of their weapons than these foster-brothers.

XXII

WHEN spring opened, the foster-brothers busked themselves for departing from home, and had thirty ships. They sailed to the east and harried in Sweden and in all parts of the Baltic. As usual, they carried on their warfare in a seeming manner, slaying vikings and pirates wherever they could find them, but leaving bondes and chapmen in peace. On the other hand, it is to be told that Otunfaxe, when he heard of the death of his brother Ufe, thought it a great loss. And of him it is to be related, that for three summers together he searched for the foster-brothers. Now it is furthermore to be related, that Bele and his men one day laid their ships near some small rocky islands, called Brenner's Isles. They cast anchor and busked themselves well. Hereupon all the three foster-brothers went ashore, and proceeded until they came to a small byre. There stood a man outside the door splitting wood; he was clad in a green cloak, and was a man of astonishing corpulency. He greeted Thorstein by name. Said Thorstein: 'We differ widely as to our faculty for recognition; you greet me by name, but I do not remember that I have ever seen you before; what is your name?' Said he: 'My name is an uncommon one. I am called Brenner. I am a son of Vifil, and a brother of your father, Viking. I was born at the time when my father was engaged in warfare, and had his home with Haloge.

I was raised on this island, and have lived here since. But have you, my nephew Thorstein, heard anything about the viking Otunfaxe?' Answered Thorstein: 'No; or what can you tell about him?' Made answer Brenner: 'This I can tell, that he has been searching for you during the last three years, and now he lies here on the other side of those islands with all his fleet; he wants to avenge his brother Ufe the Unlucky. He has forty ships, all of which are very large, and he himself is as big as a troll, and no weapons can bite him.' Said Thorstein: 'What is to be done now?' Made answer Brenner: 'I can give you no advice unless you have a chance to meet the dwarf Sindre; and moreover he will least of all be embarrassed in finding out what ought to be done.' Asked Thorstein: 'Where can I expect to find him?' Made answer Brenner: 'His home is in the island which lies near the shore, and is called the Smaller Brenner's Isle. He lives in a stone. I scarcely hope that you will be able to find him, but you are welcome here tonight.' Said Thorstein: 'Something else must be done than to keep quiet.' Then they went to their ships, and Thorstein launched a boat and rowed to the island. He went ashore alone, and when he came to a little stream, he saw two children, a boy and a girl, playing on its banks. Thorstein asked their names. The boy called himself Herraud, and the girl Herrid. Said she: 'I have lost my gold ring, and I know this will make my father, Sindre, cross, and I think I may look for punishment.' Said Thorstein: 'Here is a gold ring, which I will give you.' She accepted the gold ring and was pleased with it. Said she: 'I will give this to my father; but is there nothing that I might do that might be of service to you?' Made answer Thorstein: 'Nothing; but bring

your father here, that I may have a talk with him, and manage the matter in such a manner that he may advise me concerning those things which are of importance to me.' Answered Herrid: 'I can do this only provided my brother Herraud acts according to my will, for Sindre never refuses him anything.' Said Herraud: 'You know I take your part in everything.' Thorstein unbuckled a silver belt which he wore, and gave it him; to it was attached a beautifully ornamented knife. Said the boy: 'This is a nice present; I shall take all possible pains to promote your wish; wait here until I and my sister come back.' Thorstein did so, and after a long while the dwarf Sindre came, accompanied by the boy and his sister. Sindre greeted Thorstein heartily, and said: 'What do you want of me, Thorstein?' Made answer Thorstein: 'I want you to give me advice as to how I may conquer the viking Otunfaxe.' Answered Sindre: 'It seems to me wholly impossible for any human being to vanquish Faxe, for he is worse to deal with than anybody else, and I will advise you not to fight any battle with him, for you will only lose your men, and hence the best thing for you to do is to turn your prows away from the island tonight.' Made answer Thorstein: 'That shall never be; though I knew it before that I should lose my life, I would rather choose that than flee from danger before it has been tried.' Said Sindre: 'I see that you are a very great champion, and I suggest to you that you unload all your ships this night, bring all valuable things on shore, and that you load the ships again with wood and stones. Then busk yourself early tomorrow morning and come to them before they wake; thus you may be able to surprise them in their own tents. You need to do all this if there shall be any show for you of gaining a victory over Faxe; for I will tell you this, that so far is common iron from biting him, that he cannot even be scathed by the sword Angervadil. Here is a belt-dirk, which my daughter Herrid will give you, and thus reward you for the gold ring, and I am of the opinion that it will bite Otunfaxe if you use it skilfully. My son, Herraud, proposes this as a reward for the belt, that you shall name my name if you seem to be hard pressed. Now we must part for a while; fare you well, and good luck to you. By my power of enchanting I promise that my dises (female guardian spirits) shall always follow and assist you.' Hereupon Thorstein went to his boat and rowed to his men. Straightway afterward in the night he busked himself and brought the fee out of the ships, but put stones in them instead; and when this was done the old man Brenner came down from his byre, holding in his hand a large club which was all covered with iron and large iron spikes, and so heavy that a man with common strength could scarcely lift it from the ground. Said Brenner: 'This hand-weapon I will give you, my nephew Thorstein. You alone can manage it, on account of its weight; but yet, it will be rather light for a fight with Otunfaxe. Now it seems to me that it would be a wise measure if Angantyr would take the sword Angervadil, and you fight with this club, for, although it is no handy weapon, still it will prove fatal to many a man. Now, my nephew, I would like to be able to help you more, but I have not the opportunity.' Then Brenner went back from the shore.

XXIII

WHEN they had made ready they rowed quickly around the ness, and then they saw the place where Otunfaxe and all his naval force was lying. Without delay they sent forth a shower of stones so hard and vehemently that they slew more than a hundred men in their sleep, having taken them by surprise; but from the moment when the warriors awoke they made a powerful resistance. Then a bloody battle was fought. A large number of the men of the foster-brothers fell, for it could almost be said that Otunfaxe shot from every finger. So it went on until night set in; then ten of the foster-brothers' ships were cleared. On the second day the battle began anew, and the slaughter was no less than on the day before. They tried several times to board Faxe's ship, and every time they made great slaughter; but they never succeeded in boarding Ellide, both because Faxe defended her and because her sides were so high. But in the evening all the ships of the foster-brothers were cleared, excepting the dragon called Ufe's naut (gift). On both days they saw that two men came from the island, and that they took their positions one on one crag and the other on another, both shooting with all their might at Faxe's ship. Here they saw the dwarf Sindre, every one of whose arrows brought down a man, and in this manner a great many of Faxe's men lost their lives. The one on the other crag was Brenner, who was shooting more like a bowman out against the ships. It did happen occasionally that stones came flying over the ships, and every stone thrown by Brenner was inclined to go to the bottom, and, as a consequence of this, many of Faxe's ships sunk. Thus it happened that all his ships,

too, had been cleared, excepting Ellide. This battle took place at that time of the year when the nights are bright, and therefore they fought the whole night. Thorstein, together with Angantyr and Bele, tried to board the dragon, but there were many men left on Ellide. Faxe ran forward, against the foster-brothers, Angantyr and Bele, and a good many blows were given and received; but no iron weapons would bite Faxe, and before they had fought very long Angantyr and Bele began to receive wounds. At this moment Thorstein approached, and with his club he smote the cheek of Faxe in the way that it came handiest for him, but Faxe did not even flinch the least at the blow. Thorstein smote again, just as hard as before; and now Faxe did not like the blows, but plunged himself overboard into the sea, so that only the soles of his feet could be seen. To both Bele and Angantyr it seemed disgusting to follow him; but Thorstein ran overboard, and swam after the fleeing Faxe, who looked like a whale. Thus a long time passed until Faxe landed; but the foster-brothers fought with those men who still were left, and did not cease until they had slain all on board the dragon. Then they took a boat, and rowed ashore toward Faxe and Thorstein. But Faxe, having landed, seized a stone and threw it at Thorstein just as the latter was swimming toward the shore. He warded off the blow by diving, and swam out of the reach of the stone, which made a great splash as it fell. Faxe took up another stone, and a third one, both of which went the same way as the first one. But meanwhile the foster-brothers, Angantyr and Bele, approached. When Thorstein sprang overboard, he threw his club backwards, but Bele had taken it up, and, having now reached the spot where Otunfaxe was standing, he smote him in

the back part of the head with the club. This he did uninterrupted again, while Angantyr at the same time was pelting him with large stones. Now Faxe's skull began to ache considerably, and, not liking to receive their blows, he plunged himself from the crag down into the sea, and swam from the shore, pursued by Thorstein. Faxe, observing this, turned against Thorstein, and a wrestle between the two swimming antagonists now took place, in which there were great, fearful tussles. They were alternately drawn into the deep by each other, and yet Thorstein found out that Faxe's strength was greater than his own; and it came to pass that Faxe brought Thorstein to the bottom, and thus he lost his power of swimming. Now Thorstein, being almost sure that Faxe intended to bite his throat to pieces, said: 'How could I ever want you more than now, dwarf Sindre?' And suddenly he observed that Faxe's shoulder was seized by a grip so powerful that he soon sank to the bottom, with Thorstein upon him. Thorstein, who by this time had become very tired from the struggle, seized the belt-knife which had been given to him by Sindre, and stabbed Faxe in the breast, sinking the knife into his body up to the handle, and then slashing his belly down to the lower abdomen; but still he found that Faxe was not dead yet, for now said the latter: 'A great deed you have done, Thorstein, in putting me to death, for I have fought ninety battles, and been victorious in all, excepting this. In duels I have been the victor eighty times, so that I certainly may say I have had a holm-gang; but now I am ninety years old.' Thorstein thought it useless to let him go on prattling any longer if he could do anything to prevent it, and so he tore away from him everything that was loose within him. Now the saga goes on to tell about Angantyr and Bele, that they took a boat and rowed in it out on the sea, searching for Faxe and Thorstein, but for a long time they did not find them anywhere. At last they came to a place where the sea was mixed with blood, and quite red. They thought it must be that Faxe was at the bottom of the water, and that he had slain Thorstein, and after a while they saw some nasty thing floating upon the surface of the sea. They went nearer, and saw some large, horrible looking bowels floating there. Shortly afterward Thorstein emerged from the water, but so exhausted and outdone that he could not keep himself afloat. Then they rowed over to him, and dragged him on board. At this time there was but little hope of his life, and still he was not much wounded, but the flesh of his body was almost torn from his bones into knots. They went away and procured some relief for him, after which he soon came to his senses. They went back to the islands, and made a search of the battle-field for the slain; but only thirty men were found fit to be healed. Then they went to the old man Brenner, thanking him for his assistance. Thorstein went to the Smaller Brenner's Isle to call on the dwarf Sindre, to whom he made splendid presents, and thus they parted in great friendship. Thorstein got the dragon Ellide as his lot of the booty, while Bele got Ufe's naut, and Angantyr as much gold and silver as he wished. Thorstein gave his uncle Brenner all those ships which they could not bring away with them. With three ships they left and went back to Sogn, where they spent the winter.

XXIV

IN the spring they set out for warfare again. Angantyr asked whither they should turn their prows, saying that he thought the Baltic had already been cleared of vikings. Said king Bele: 'Let us then take our course into the western waters, for we have never been there a harrying before.' So they did, and having reached the Orkneys, they went ashore, and waged war, destroying the inhabited parts of these islands by fire and plundering the fee; and so fearfully did they carry on their depredations that all living things fled for fear of them. Herraud was the jarl who ruled the islands. When he heard of their depredations he gathered an army to meet them, and marched by day and by night until he found them at an island called Pap Isle. Here it came to a battle between them, and their troops were equal. For two days they fought in such a manner that it could not be seen which party would be victorious. At last the slaughter began to lean to the disadvantage of Herraud, whose ships were cleared, so that the brothers succeeded in boarding them, and finally jarl Herraud fell, together with the most of his men. Hereupon they made expeditions through all the islands, which they subjugated, and then busked themselves for the home journey. King Bele offered to make Thorstein jarl of all the islands, but the latter declined, saying: 'I would rather be a herser, and not part with you, than have the name of jarl, and live far away from you.'

Then he offered Angantyr the jarlship of those islands, which offer was accepted. The latter became jarl, and was to pay an annual tribute. Afterward they returned home to Sogn, where they stayed the next winter, keeping their men well, both as to weapons and clothes. And now none were thought to be superior to the foster-brothers. Children were granted to them; the sons of Bele were called Helge and Halfdan, and his daughter was Ingeborg; she was the youngest of the children. Thorstein had a son, who was named Fridthjof. Harald grew up in the island with Grim, but when he had reached the age of maturity he set out a harrying and became a most noted man, although he is not much spoken of in this saga. He kept his nickname, being called Harald Kesia, and a large family is descended from him. Thorstein, Bele, Grim and Harald remained friends as long as they lived.

XXV

NOW we must return to Jokul, Njorfe's son, who ruled the uplands after the death of Njorfe and Viking. They had preserved their friendship well until their death. Jokul won ships and fee, and was a daring viking, treating his soldiers fairly well, but no better. A few years passed in such a manner that he was the most noted viking, harrying the most of the time in the waters of the Baltic. Thorstein and Bele had not been at home long before they busked themselves for harrying expeditions, and sailing first down along the coast of the country, then through the Sound, they harried in Saxland during the summer, and got a great booty, consisting of gold and silver, and many other costly things. Afterward they intended to sail home, which they did, and having reached the mouth of Lim Fjord, they were overtaken by a violent storm,

which carried them out into the sea, and in a short time the ships were separated. Then the sea began to break over the ships from both sides, and all the men were engaged in baling out the water. And it came to pass that this storm drove the dragon Ellide, tossed by the waves, ashore alone at Borgund's Holm. At the same time Jokul also landed there with ten ships, all thoroughly equipped both as to weapons and crews. And now, as might be imagined, Jokul attacked Thorstein and his men. Thorstein was poorly prepared, for he and his crew were very much exhausted from hard work, and from being tossed about on the sea. A severe and bloody battle was fought, and Jokul, being very vehement, kept cheering his men on, telling them that they would never have a better chance to conquer Thorstein; and, said he, it will be an everlasting shame upon us if he escapes now. Then they attacked Thorstein and his men, not letting up until all his men had fallen, so that nobody but Thorstein alone remained standing on the dragon; but still he defended himself bravely, so that for a long time they could not give him a single wound. At last, however, it came to pass that they came so near to him that they could stab him with their spears; but the most of them he cut out of his reach, for the sword Angervadil bit as keenly as ever. Then Jokul made a desperate attack, and stabbed Thorstein with his spear through the thigh. At the same moment Thorstein dealt Jokul a blow, hitting his arm below the elbow, and cutting the hand off. Meanwhile they succeeded in surrounding Thorstein with shields and capturing him. But it was near night, so that they thought it was too late to put him to death, and so fetters were put on his feet, his hands were tied with a bow-string, and twelve men were set to watch him during the night. When all had been brought ashore excepting these twelve men, together with Thorstein, he said: 'Which do you prefer, that you amuse me, or that I amuse you?' They said that he could not care much for amusement now, as he was to die immediately on the morrow. Now Thorstein, finding himself in close quarters, conceived a plan of escaping, and in a low, whispering voice he said: 'At what other time could I need you more than just now, my dear fellow Sindre, had not all our friendship already been broken off?' Then darkness came upon the watchmen, and they all fell asleep. Thorstein saw Sindre going along the ship, approaching him, and saying: 'You are in close quarters, my dear fellow Thorstein, and it certainly is high time to help you.' He blew open the lock, then he cut the bow-string off from his hands; and Thorstein, who thus had become free, now seized his sword, for he knew where he had left it, and, turning against the watchmen, he killed them all. Hereupon, Sindre disappeared, but Thorstein took a boat and rowed ashore, and went home to Sogn. This meeting with Bele was a very happy one, and to the latter it seemed as if he had recovered Thorstein from the domains of Hel (death). Early the next morning (after the battle) Jokul awoke, happy in the thought that he was about to take the prisoner and kill him; but when they came to the place where they had left him, the prisoner was gone, and the watchmen dead. This was to them a very great loss. Jokul turned his prows homeward, greatly dissatisfied with his voyage, having lost Thorstein, and received scars that could never be healed. Henceforth he was called Jokul the One-handed. The foster-brothers, king Bele and Thorstein, gathered an army and

went to the uplands, sending a message to Jokul, and preparing a battle-field for him. Jokul gathered men, although, on account of their friendship with Thorstein, many of his subjects sat at home, and thus, getting only a few, he durst not engage in battle, but fled out of his land, and went to Valland to his brother-in-law, Vilhjalm. The latter gave him a third part of his kingdom to rule. King Bele and Thorstein conquered the uplands, whereupon they returned home and kept quiet. Some time later there came men from Valland to meet Thorstein. They had been sent out by Jokul. Their errand was to offer Thorstein, in the name of Jokul, terms of peace. They were to have a meeting in Lim Fjord, to which both should come with three ships each, and there they should settle their dispute. Thorstein was very much pleased with this offer, confessing that it was contrary to his wish that he had had troubles with Jokul, saying that he had entered into them unwillingly on Njorfe's account, and on account of the latter's friendship with Viking. Now this was agreed upon. The ambassadors returned home, but in the summer time Thorstein busked himself for going abroad, taking with him Ellide and two other ships. To Bele this voyage did not seem a hopeful one, for he looked upon Jokul as a treacherous and faithless man. He advised Thorstein to send spies ahead, and find out whether everything was done faithfully on Jokul's part, and having found this out, they should return and meet him in the Sound. They did so, and came back, reporting that Jokul and his party were lying at anchor in Lim Fjord, and keeping perfectly quiet. So they proceeded on their voyage till they reached the fjord. Here they held a meeting in the place agreed upon, and came to mutually satisfactory terms, on the conditions that the loss of men, the wounds and the blows, should be considered even on both sides, but Jokul should get his kingdom back, and not be tributary to anybody. Thorstein's kingdom in the uplands should fall to Jokul's lot, in compensation for the loss of his hand. On these conditions they were to be fully reconciled. Then Jokul went home to his kingdom, and kept quiet. Thorstein and Bele went home to Sogn, settled in their kingdoms, and made an end to all warfares. Ingeborg, Thorstein's wife, had already died, and Ingeborg, Bele's daughter, had her name. Fridthjof grew up with his father. Thorstein had a daughter named Vefreyja, who at this point of our saga had reached the age of maturity, for she was begotten in the cave of Skellinefja, and there she was born too. In wisdom she was like her mother. She got Angervadil after the death of her father, Thorstein, and many excellent men are descended from him. By all, Thorstein was considered the most distinguished and most excellent man of his time. With these contents, we now finish the saga of Thorstein, Viking's son, and it is a most amusing one.

The Saga of Fridthjof the Bold

I

THE beginning of this saga is, that king Bele ruled over the Sogn fylke. He had three children: a son, who was called Helge, another by name Halfdan, and a daughter called Ingeborg, a fair looking woman, of great wisdom, and the foremost of the king's children. On the coast bordering the fjord on the west side there was a large byre, called Baldershage (Balder's Meads). There was a Place of Peace and a great temple inclosed with high wooden pales. Many gods were there, yet none of them was such a favourite as Balder; and so jealous were the heathen people of this place, that no harm should be done therein, either to beasts or to men; and no dealings must there take place between men and women. The place where the king dwelt was called Syrstrand, but on the other side of the fjord was a byre called Framness.

There dwelt a man named Thorstein, the son of Viking. His byre was over against the dwelling of the king. With his wife, Thorstein had a son, by name Fridthjof, a man taller and stronger than anybody else, and even from his youth furnished with very unusual prowess. He was called Fridthjof the Bold, and so much was he beloved that all men prayed for his welfare. The children of the king were still young when their mother died. Hilding was the name of a good bonde in Sogn. He offered to foster the king's daughter, and so she was brought up in his house well and carefully. She was called Ingeborg the Fair. Fridthjof was also fostered by the bonde Hilding, and thus Ingeborg was his foster-sister, and both of them were peerless among children. King Bele growing old, his personal property began to ebb away from his hands. Thorstein ruled over the third part of his kingdom, and from that man Bele got more aid than from any other source. Every third year Thorstein invited the king to a very costly banquet, while the king, on the other hand, gave a feast to Thorstein the other two years. At an early age Helge, Bele's son, turned to offering to the gods, and yet neither he nor his brother was much beloved. Thorstein had a ship called Ellide, rowed on each side by fifteen oars, furnished with bow-shaped stem and stern, and strong-built like an ocean-going vessel, and its sides were clamped with iron. So strong was Fridthjof, that he, at the bow of the ship, rowed with two oars thirteen ells long, while everywhere else there were two men at each oar. Fridthjof was considered peerless among young men of that time, and the sons of the king were jealous, because he was praised more than themselves. Now king Bele was taken ill, and when he was rapidly approaching death he sent for

his sons and said to them: 'This illness will be my bane, but this I will bid you, that you keep friendship with the friends that I have had, for it seems to me that you are inferior to Thorstein and his son Fridthjof in all things, both in good counsel and bravery. You shall raise a mound over me.' Hereupon Bele died. Soon afterward Thorstein also was taken sick, and then he said to Fridthjof: 'This will I bid you, my son, that you govern your temper and yield to the sons of the king, for this is fitting on account of their dignity, and besides it seems to me that your future promises much good. I wish to be buried in a how opposite the how of king Bele, on this side of the fjord, close by the sea, so that it may be an easy thing to shout to one another about things that are about to happen.' Bjorn and Asmund were named the foster-brothers of Fridthjof; both of them were large and strong men. Shortly after this Thorstein died. He was buried in a how according to his request, but Fridthjof took his land and all his personal property after him.

II

FRIDTHJOF became the most famous man, and the bravest in all dangers. His foster-brother, Bjorn, he valued most, but Asmund served both of them. The best thing he got of his father's heritage was the ship Ellide, and another costly thing was a gold ring, and a dearer one was not to be found in all Norway. So bounteous a man was Fridthjof that he was commonly said to be no less honourable than the sons of the king, excepting their royal dignity. On account of this they showed great coldness and enmity toward Fridthjof, and they could not easily bear to hear him spoken of as superior to themselves; and, furthermore, they seemed to have seen that their sister, Ingeborg, and Fridthjof had fallen into mutual love. Now the time came when the kings had to attend a banquet at Fridthjof's, at Framness, and, as usual, he entertained everybody more splendidly than they were wont to be entertained. Ingeborg was also present at this feast, and Fridthjof frequently talked with her. Said the king's daughter to him: 'You have a good gold ring.' Said Fridthjof: 'That is true.' Hereupon, the brothers went home, and their envy of Fridthjof grew. Shortly afterward Fridthjof became very sad. Bjorn, his foster-brother, asked him what the matter was. Fridthjof answered that he had in mind to woo Ingeborg; for, said he, 'though my title is less than that of her brothers, still I am not inferior to them in personal worth.' Said Bjorn: 'Let us do so.' Then Fridthjof, in company with a few men, went to see the brothers. The kings were sitting on their father's how, when Fridthjof greeted them courteously. Thereupon he presented his request, saying that he prayed for their sister, Ingeborg, Bele's daughter. Said the kings: 'You do not show great wisdom in making this request, thinking that we will give her in marriage to a man who is without dignity. We therefore most positively refuse to give our consent.' Said Fridthjof: 'Then my errand is quickly done; but this shall be given in return, that hereafter I shall never give you my help, though you may be in want of it.' They said they did not care about it at all. Then Fridthjof returned home, and got back his cheerful mind.

III

THERE was a king, by name Ring, who ruled over Ring-ric, which also is a part of Norway. He was a mighty fylke-king, of great ability, but at this time somewhat advanced in age. Spoke he to his men: 'I have heard that the sons of Bele have broken off their friendship with Fridthjof, a man of quite uncommon excellence. Now I will send some men to the kings, and offer them this choice – either they must become subject and tributary to me, or I will equip an army against them; and I think it will be easy to capture their kingdom, for they are not my peers either in forces or in wisdom, and yet it would be a great honour to me in my old age to put them to death.' Hereupon king Ring's messengers left, and, meeting the brothers, Helge and Halfdan, in Sogn, they spoke to them as follows: 'This message does king Ring send you, that you must either pay a tribute to him, or he will come and harry your kingdom.' They made answer that they were unwilling to learn in their youth that which they had no mind to know in their old age, namely, to serve him with shame; and now, said they, 'We shall gather all the army that we may be able to get together.' And so they did; but, as it seemed to them that their army would be small, they sent Hilding's foster-father to Fridthjof, asking him to come and help the kings. Fridthjof was sitting at the knave-play (chess) when Hilding came. Said Hilding: 'Our kings send you their greetings, and request your help for the battle with king Ring, who is going to invade their kingdom with arrogance and wrong.' Fridthjof answered nothing, but said to Bjorn, with whom he was playing: 'There is an open place there, foster-brother, and you will not be able to mend it; but I will attack the red piece, and see whether it can be saved.' Said Hilding then again: 'King Helge bade me say this to you, Fridthjof, that you should go into this warfare together with them, or you might look for a severe treatment from them when they come back.' Said Bjorn then: 'There is a choice between two, foster-brother, and there are two moves by which you may escape.' Said Fridthjof: 'Then I think it advisable to attack the knave first; and yet the double game is sure to be doubtful.' No other answer to his errand did Hilding get, and so, without delay, he went back and told the kings what Fridthjof had said. They asked Hilding what meaning he could make out of those words. Answered he: 'When he spoke of the open place, he thought, in my opinion, of leaving his place in your expedition open; but when he pretended to attack the red piece, I think he by this meant your sister, Ingeborg; watch her, therefore, as well as you can. But when I threatened him with severe treatment from you, Bjorn considered it a choice between two, but Fridthjof said the knave must be attacked first, and by this he meant king Ring.' Then the kings busked themselves for departure, but before they went they brought Ingeborg to Baldershage, and eight maidens with her. Said they that Fridthjof would not be so daring that he would go thither to meet her, for nobody is so rash as to injure anybody there. But the brothers went south to Jadar, and met king Ring in Sokn-Sound. What most of all made king Ring angry was that the brothers had said that they thought it a shame to fight with a man so old that he was unable to mount his horse without help.

IV

WHEN the kings had gone away Fridthjof took his robes of state, and put his good gold ring on his hand; then the foster-brothers went down to the sea and launched Ellide. Said Bjorn: 'Whither shall we now turn the prow, foster-brother?' Answered Fridthjof: 'To Baldershage, and amuse ourselves with Ingeborg.' Said Bjorn: 'It is not a proper thing to do, to provoke the gods.' Said Fridthjof: 'Yet that risk shall now be run; besides, I rate the favour of Ingeborg of more account than that of Balder.' Hereupon they rowed over the fjord, walked up to Baldershage and entered Ingeborg's bower, where she sat, together with eight maidens, and they, too, were eight. But when they came there all the place was covered with cloth of pall and other fine woven stuff. Then Ingeborg arose and said: 'Why are you so overbold, Fridthjof, that you have come here without the consent of my brothers, and thus provoke the wrath of the gods?' Made answer Fridthjof: 'However this may be, I consider your love of more account than the wrath of the gods.' Answered Ingeborg: 'You shall be welcome here, and all your men.' Then she made room for him to sit at her side, and drank his toast of the best wine, and they sat and were merry together. Then Ingeborg, seeing the gold ring on his hand, asked whether he was the owner of that precious thing. Fridthjof said it was his. She praised the ring very much. Said Fridthjof: 'I will give you the ring if you promise not to part with it, and will send it to me when you no longer care to keep it, and with it we pledge our troth and love to each other.'

With this pledging of troth they exchanged rings. Fridthjof spent many nights at Baldershage, and every day he went over there now and then to be merry with Ingeborg.

V

NOW it is to be told of the brothers, that they met king Ring, who had more forces than they; then some people went between them, trying to bring about an agreement, so that there should be no battle. King Ring said he was willing to settle with them, on the condition that the brothers submit to him and give him their sister, Ingeborg the Fair, in marriage, together with the third part of all their possessions. The kings consented to this, for they saw that they had to do with a force far superior to their own. This peace was firmly established by oaths, and the wedding was to be in Sogn, when king Ring came to meet his betrothed. The brothers fared home again with their troops, right ill content with the result. When Fridthjof thought the time had come when the brothers might be expected home, he said to the daughter of the king: 'Well and handsomely you have treated us, nor has the bonde Balder been angry with us. But as soon as you know that your kings have come home, then spread your bed-sheets on the hall of the goddesses, for that is the highest of all the houses in this place, and we can easily see it from our byre.' Said the king's daughter: 'You have not followed the example of other men in this matter, but we certainly must welcome our friends when you come to us.' Then Fridthjof went home, and early the next morning he went

out-doors, and when he came in again he sang:

Tell I must,
Our good people,
That our pleasure trips
Wholly are ended;
Men shall no more
Go aboard the ships,
For now are the sheets
Spread out to bleach.

So they went out, and saw that all the hall of the goddesses was thatched with bleached linen. Said Bjorn then: 'Now the kings must have come home, and for us I think there will be but a short peace; to me it seems advisable that we gather folks together.' This was done, and many men flocked together there. Soon the brothers heard of the ways of Fridthjof, and of his men and forces. Said king Helge then: 'It seems a wonder to me that Balder must endure every disgrace from Fridthjof. Now I will send messengers to him, and know what kind of atonement he is willing to offer us, or else he is to be driven from the land, for I do not see that we have men enough at our command now to fight with him.' Fridthjof's friends and his foster-father, Hilding, brought the message to him. Said they: 'The kings ask as an atonement from you, Fridthjof, that you go and collect the tribute from the Orkneys, which has never been paid since the death of Bele, for they are in want of the money just now, as they are about to give their sister Ingeborg in marriage, and a large amount of wealth with her.' Made answer Fridthjof: 'The only thing urging peace between us is regard for our deceased relatives, but the brothers will show us no trustiness. But this I will reserve, that all our possessions shall be left in peace during our absence. This was promised and bound with an oath. Now Fridthjof made preparations for his voyage, choosing his men in reference to their bravery and ability to render service. The company consisted of eighteen men. Fridthjof's men asked him if he would not before setting out go to king Helge and make peace with him, and pray Balder to take his wrath away from him. Said Fridthjof: 'I make a solemn vow that I shall never ask for peace from king Helge.' Hereupon he went aboard Ellide, and so they sailed out of the Sogn-Fjord. But when Fridthjof had departed from home, said king Halfdan to his brother Helge as follows: 'Our rule would be better and greater if Fridthjof was paid for his misdoings. Let us burn up his byre, and bring such a storm upon him and his men that they may perish.' Helge said this was a thing to be done. Thereupon they burnt up the whole byre at Framness, and robbed it of all its fee. Then they sent for two witch-wives, Heid and Hamglom, and gave them fee to send upon Fridthjof and his men so mighty a tempest that they should all be wrecked. So the witches sang their songs of witchcraft, and ascended the witch-scaffold with sorcery and incantations.

VI

BUT when Fridthjof and his men had gotten out of the Sogn-Fjord there fell upon them a violent storm and a great tempest,

and the sea rolled heavily. The ship sped on swiftly, for it glided smoothly over the waters, and had an excellent form for breasting the sea. Sang Fridthjof then:

My tarred horse of the sea
I let swim out of Sogn,
While the maids were drinking mead
In the midst of Baldershage.
The tempest now increases,
Farewell, my brides, I bid you,
Who have a mind to love us,
Though Ellide should be filled.

Said Bjorn: 'It would be well if you could find something else to do than to sing about the maids of Baldershage.' Made answer Fridthjof: 'My songs will not give out so soon, though.' Then they were driven northward to the sounds near the islands called the Solunds. And now the storm had reached its highest pitch. Sang then Fridthjof:

High now the sea is swelling;
The waves and clouds unite,
Old spells are the causes
That call forth the breakers;
With Æger shall I not
Contend in the tempest.
Let the ice-clad Solunds
Shelter our people!

Then they stood toward the islands that are called the Solunds, and intended to stop there; and now the storm suddenly abated. Then they took another course, and turned their prow away from the islands, having fair prospects for the voyage, for they had favourable wind for awhile; but the fair wind soon freshened into a gale. Sang Fridthjof then:

> In former days
> At Framness
> I rowed to meet
> My Ingeborg.
> Now I shall sail
> In the tempest cold,
> Making the horse of the wave
> Smoothly speed on.

And when they had sped before the wind far into the sea the waters began to be violently agitated again, and a gale blew up, accompanied by so great a snow-storm that the stem could not be seen from the stern, but the seas rushed over the ship so that the water had to be baled out constantly. Sang Fridthjof then:

> The waves are hid from sight,
> For witch-wrought is the weather.
> Heroes we of a well-famed band
> Far out on the sea have come.
> Stand we now all –

Disappeared have the Solunds –
Eighteen men a-baling
And Ellide sustaining.

Said Bjorn: 'Varied will be his fortunes who fares far.' 'That is certainly so,' said Fridthjof, and sang:

Helge it is who causes
The rime-maned waves to swell.
This is not like kissing
The bride so fair in Baldershage;
Otherwise quite does love me
Ingeborg than the king.
I know no greater happiness
Than her wishes to fulfil.

Said Bjorn: 'Maybe she is looking to something higher for you than your present position, and this is not unpleasant to know.' Said Fridthjof: 'Now is the time to test good companions, though it would be more agreeable to be in Baldershage.' They busked themselves bravely, for valiant men had gathered there, and the ship was the best that ever had been in the Northlands. Sang Fridthjof then this stave:

The waves are hid from sight,
Far west in the sea we are come.
Seems the ocean to me
Like embers all blazing.

High dash the breakers;
Hows are tossed up
By the swan-feathered billows.
On the rising ridges
Now Ellide rides.

Now huge seas were shipped, so that all had to be baling out water. Sang Fridthjof:

Much must there now be drunk
To me by the maid's fair lips
East, where the sheets lay bleaching,
If it shall make me sink
'Neath the swan-feathered waves.

Said Bjorn: 'Do you think the maids of Sogn will shed many tears for you when you are dead?' Made answer Fridthjof: 'That certainly comes into my mind.' Then a huge sea broke over the bow of the ship, so that streams of water rushed in; but this saved them, that the ship was so excellent and the crew so hardy. Sang Bjorn then a stave:

It seems not that a widow
To you does drink,
Nor that the ring-keeper fair
Bids you draw near to her.
Salt are our eyes,
Soaked in the brine;

Our strong arms are failing,
Our eyelids are sore.

Answered Asmund: 'It does not matter though you do try your arms somewhat, for you did not pity us when we rubbed our eyes every morning when you rose so early to go to Baldershage.' Said Fridthjof: 'Well, why do you not make a stave, Asmund?' 'That shall not be,' said Asmund, but still he sang this stave:

Tight was the tug round the mast,
When the seas broke over the ship;
I alone 'gainst eight men
Within board had to work.
Better was it to bring
Breakfast to the maiden's bower
Than to be baling out
Ellide Mid the roaring waves.

Said Fridthjof, laughing: 'You do not speak of your help in lower terms than it deserves, nevertheless you now showed something of the thrall-blood in you, when you were willing to be a table-waiter.' The storm still kept increasing, so that the breakers that roared round the ship seemed to the men who were on board more like huge peaks and mountains than like waves. Sang Fridthjof then:

On cushioned seat I sat
In Baldershage,
Singing the songs I knew

For the king's fair daughter.
Now am I really
To Rán's bed going,
And another shall own
My Ingeborg.

Said Bjorn: 'Great fear is now before us, foster-brother, and your words betoken anxiety, and that is too bad for such a brave fellow as you are.' Said Fridthjof: 'There is neither fear nor anxiety, though ditties are made of our pleasure voyages, but it may be that they are spoken of oftener than need be, but most men would think themselves nearer to death than life if they were in our place.' He answered with a stave:

That did I get to my gain;
With the maidens eight
Of Ingeborg did I, not you,
Succeed in negotiations.
At Baldershage we laid
Bright rings together;
Nor far away was then
The warder [i.e., Balder] of Halfdan's land.

Said Bjorn: 'Such things as are already done, foster brother, we must be content with. Now the seas dashed over the ship so violently that the bulwarks and both the sheets were broken, and four men were washed overboard and all were lost.' Sang Fridthjof then:

Broken are both the sheets
Mid the ocean's great waves;
Four swains did sink
In the sea so deep.

Said Fridthjof: 'Reasonable it now seems to me that some of our men will go to Rán; but in my opinion we will not be considered fit to be sent thither unless we may come there busked like men, and it therefore seems good to me that every one of us have some gold on him.' Then he cut the ring, Ingeborg's gift, asunder, distributed the pieces among his men, and sang this stave:

Before we are lost by Æger,
Asunder shall be hewed the ring,
By the wealthy father of Halfdan owned.
Red as it is,
Gold shall glitter on the guests,
If of guesting we have need,
That will be fitting
For men of might
In the midst of Rán's halls.

Said Bjorn then: 'Now it is not to be looked for with any certainty that we come there, although it is not unlikely.' At this moment Fridthjof and his men observed that the ship was gliding over the waves very rapidly, but before them was a wholly unknown sea, and it was growing dark on all sides, so that no one could see the stem or stern from the middle of the ship, and the darkness was accompanied by sea-spray, storm, frost, snow and piercing cold. Then Fridthjof climbed the mast, and when he came down again said he to his companions: 'A wondrous sight I have seen: a large whale was swimming round the ship, and I have no doubt we must have come near to some land, and that this whale intends to keep us from reaching it. King Helge, I think, does not deal kindly with us, and he has undoubtedly sent us anything but a friendly messenger. I saw two women on the back of the whale, and they, methinks, cause this fearful tempest by witchcraft and sorcery of the worst sort. Now let us try whether our good luck or their witchcraft is more powerful, and you shall steer ashore as straightly as possible, but I shall smite these monsters with beams.' Sang he then this stave:

> Witches two
> On the wave I see,
> Has them hither
> Helge sent.
> Their backs shall Ellide
> Cut in twain
> E'er she her voyage
> Completed has.

It is said that the ship Ellide had by enchantment gotten the power of understanding human speech. Said Bjorn then: 'Now men can see the disposition of the brothers toward us.' Then Bjorn took the command of the ship; but Fridthjof seized a forked

beam, ran to the prow and sang this stave:

Hail, Ellide!
Leap on the wave!
Break of the witches
The teeth and brow!
The cheeks and jaw-bones
Of the cursed woman,
One foot or both
Of this horrible witch!

Then he shot a fork at one of the ham-leapers (skin-changers), but the beak of Ellide struck the back of the other, and the backs of both were broken; but the whale dove down and swam away, and they saw him no more. Now the weather grew calmer, but the ship was waterlogged, and then Fridthjof called to his men requesting them to bale the ship dry. Bjorn said that this work was not needed. Whereto made answer Fridthjof: 'Have a care, foster-brother, and do not fall into despair; it has, you know, heretofore been the custom of brave men to give aid as long as possible, no matter what the result may be.' Fridthjof sang this stave:

My brave men! you need not
Have fear of death.
Exult with joy,
My thanes!
For this my dreams

Full well do know,
That I shall own
My Ingeborg.

Having then baled the ship dry, and being near land, a rainy wind still blew against them. Then Fridthjof took two oars, seated himself in the foremost part of the prow and rowed rather vigorously. Thereupon the weather cleared off, and now they saw that they had gotten out of the sound of Effia, and there they landed. The crew were very much exhausted, but so stout was Fridthjof that he bore eight men over the fore-shore; Bjorn bore two, but Asmund one. Sang Fridthjof then:

Up to the hearth
Myself did bear
My brave men, exhausted
By the raging snow-storm.
Now on the sand
The sail I have brought;
With the might of the sea
It's not easy to deal.

VII

ANGANTYR was in Effia when Fridthjof landed there with his men. It was his custom when he drank that some man should sit at the watch-window of his drinking-hall, and look toward the

wind and keep watch there. This man was to drink from a horn, and whenever one horn was emptied by him another was filled. He who was keeping watch at the time when Fridthjof landed was called Hallvard. Hallvard saw the coming of Fridthjof and his men, and sang this stave:

In the violent storm
I see on board Ellide
Six men a-baling
And seven a-rowing.
The man in the prow,
Bending over the oars,
Is like Fridthjof the Bold,
The valiant in battle.

And when he had drunk from the horn he threw it in through the window, and said to the woman who gave him drink:

Thou fair-walking woman!
Take from the floor
The horn turned over,
Which I have emptied!
Men I see on the sea,
Exhausted by storm and rain,
Who our help may need
Ere the harbour they reach.

The jarl heard what Hallvard said, and asked for tidings.

Said Hallvard: 'Some men have landed here; they are quite exhausted, but I think they are good fellows, and one of them is so doughty that he is carrying the other men ashore.' Said the jarl then: 'Go to meet them, and receive them in a seemly manner, if it should happen to be Fridthjof, son of my friend, the herser Thorstein; he is a most excellent man in respect to every accomplishment.' Then took up the word the man who was named Atle, a great viking, and said he: 'Now it shall be found out whether Fridthjof, as it is said, has made a solemn vow never to be the first in praying for peace from anybody.' Together with Atle there were ten bad and ambitious men, who often went into berserks-gang. When they met Fridthjof they took their weapons. Said Atle then: 'Now it seems good, Fridthjof, that you turn this way, for as eagles fight face to face with their claws, so must we also, Fridthjof; and moreover, now is the time for you to keep your word, and not be the first to ask for peace.' Fridthjof turned to meet them, and sang this stave:

Succeed shall you never
In cowing us down,
You fainting cowards,
Dwellers of these isles!
Rather would I go
Alone to fight
With you men ten
Than sue for peace.

Then Hallvard came to them and said: 'The jarl desires me to bid you all welcome, and no one shall insult you.' Fridthjof said

that he heartily accepted this greeting of welcome, and yet he was prepared to take either peace or war. Thereupon they went to call on the jarl, who received Fridthjof and all his men kindly. They spent the winter with the jarl, and were held in great honour by him; the latter frequently made questions about their voyages. This stave sang Bjorn:

During ten whole days,
And eight days more,
We, fellows so merry,
Continued a-baling,
While billows dashed o'er us
From both sides.

Made answer the jarl: 'Greatly has king Helge vexed you, and evil are such kings as do nothing but put people to death by witchcraft; but I know, Fridthjof,' said Angantyr, 'what your errand hither is; you are sent hither to gather tribute, and thereto I can speedily give the answer, that king Helge shall have no tribute from me, but you may have as much fee from me as you please, and you may call it tribute or anything else you have a mind to.' Fridthjof said he would accept the fee.

VIII

NOW it shall be told what came to pass in Norway after Fridthjof had gone abroad. The brothers burned up all the byre at Framness.

But while the weird sisters were performing their spells they fell down from the witch-scaffold on which they were seated, and both of them broke their backs. This autumn king Ring came north to Sogn to have his wedding, and a great feast was prepared for his nuptials with Ingeborg. Said king Ring to Ingeborg: 'Whence has come that excellent ring that you wear on your hand?' She said her father had been its owner. Answered he: 'It is a gift of Fridthjof; take it off your hand straightway, for you shall not be in want of gold when you come to Alfheim.' Then she handed the ring to Helge's wife, and bade her give it to Fridthjof when he came back. King Ring then went home with his wife, and his love of her was exceedingly great.

IX

THE next spring Fridthjof departed from the Orkneys, and parted with Angantyr on the most friendly terms. Hallvard went with Fridthjof. But when they came to Norway they learned that his byre had been burnt up, and when Fridthjof came to Framness he said:

Stout fellows, we
Formerly did drink
At Framness
With my father.
Now burnt I see
That same byre;

Repay must I
The king's ill deeds.

Then he consulted his men as to what was now to be done, but they bade him look to that himself; whereunto he made answer that he would first hand over the tribute. Afterward they rowed the boat over and came to Syrstrand. There they learn that the kings were at Baldershage, sacrificing to the dises (goddesses). Bjorn and Fridthjof then went up thither; and the latter bade Hallvard, Asmund and the other men break in pieces all the ships, large and small, that were to be found thereabout. So they did. Fridthjof and his men then went to the door of Baldershage. Fridthjof wanted to enter. Bjorn bade him go warily, as he wanted to go in alone. Fridthjof bade Bjorn remain outside and keep watch while he entered. Sang he then this stave:

Alone will I go
And enter the byre:
Little help do I need
The kings to find.
You shall throw fire
On the byre of the kings,
If I do not come
Back tonight.

Said Bjorn: 'That stave was well sung.' Then Fridthjof went in and saw that there were but a few people in the hall of the dises; the kings were there at the time sacrificing, and sat drinking. Fire was burning on the floor, and the wives of the kings sat at the fires and warmed the gods, whereas other women were anointing the gods and wiping them with napkins. Fridthjof went before king Helge and said: 'Here you have the tribute.' Herewith he swung the purse wherein was the silver, and threw it at his nose so violently that two teeth were broken out of his mouth, and he fell into a swoon in his high seat; but Halfdan caught him, so that he did not fall into the fire. Sang Fridthjof then this stave:

Take here your tribute,
King of men!
Take it with your foreteeth
Lest more you demand.
At the bottom of this belg
You find silver abounding,
O'er which have ruled together
Bjorn and I.

There were but few men in the room, for in another place there was drinking going on. But as Fridthjof walked over the floor toward the door, he saw that goodly ring on the hand of Helge's wife while she was warming Balder at the fire. Fridthjof took after the ring, but it stuck fast to her hand, and so he dragged her along the floor toward the door, and then Balder fell into the fire. But when Halfdan's wife caught after her quickly, the god that she had been warming also fell into the fire. The flame now blazed up around both the gods, as they had previously been anointed,

and thence it ran up into the roof, so that the whole house was wrapped in flames. Fridthjof got hold of the ring before he went out. Asked Bjorn then what had taken place during his visit in the house. But Fridthjof held the ring up and sang this stave:

> A blow received Helge;
> Smote the purse the villain's nose;
> Down fell the brother of Halfdan
> In the midst of the high seat.
> Balder had to burn,
> But first got I the ring.
> Then from the fire-place I
> Fearlessly wended my way.

People say that Fridthjof flung a flaming fire-brand at the roof, so that all the house was wrapped in flames, and that he then sang this stave:

> Wend we our way to the strand!
> Then let our aims be high!
> For the blue flame is bickering
> In the midst of Baldershage.
> Hereupon they went down to the sea.

X

WHEN king Helge had come to his senses he gave orders to follow

quickly after Fridthjof and kill him and all of his companions. That man, said he, has forfeited his life, as he has spared no Place of Peace. Now the trumpet was blown, and all the king's men came together; and when they came out to the hall, they saw that it stood in flames. King Halfdan and some of his men went to the fire, but king Helge followed after Fridthjof and his men. The latter had already got on board their ships and were lying on their oars. Helge and his men found that all their ships had been damaged, so they were forced to row ashore again, and lost some men. Then king Helge grew so angry that he became stark mad. Thereupon, with an arrow on the string, he stretched his bow and intended to shoot at Fridthjof, but he bent his bow with so much force that both ends of it suddenly snapped off. When Fridthjof saw this, he seized two of Ellide's oars and plied them so mightily that both of them broke. Sang he then this stave:

Kissed I the young Ingeborg,
Bele's daughter,
In Baldershage.
Thus shall the oars
Of Ellide
Both be broken
Like Helge's bows.

After this the wind began to blow out of the inner part of the fjord, so they hoisted the sails and sailed on. Fridthjof said to his men that they might busk themselves not to stay there very long. Afterward they sailed out of Sogn. Sang Fridthjof then this stave:

Sailed we out of Sogn,
Here sailed we a short time ago;
When flames consumed the byre
My father left to me.
But now in the midst of Baldershage
The flames have begun to blaze.
I now am an outlaw, for sooth
I know that it has been sworn.

Said Bjorn to Fridthjof: 'What shall we do now?' 'Foster-brother,' said Fridthjof, 'I shall not remain here in Norway; I will try the life of warriors, and go on viking expeditions.' Then they explored islands and skerries during the summer, and thus gained for themselves fee and fame; but in the autumn they repaired to the Orkneys, where they were heartily welcomed by Angantyr, and they spent the winter there. But when Fridthjof had left Norway the kings held a thing, and declared Fridthjof an outlaw in all their realms, and made all his possessions their own. King Halfdan settled at Framness, and rebuilt the byre which had been burnt down; and likewise they restored the whole Baldershage, but it took a long time before the fire was put out. That which most touched the heart of Helge was that the gods had been burnt up, and it cost much to build Baldershage up again as it had been before. Sat king Helge now at Syrstrand.

XI

FRIDTHJOF was successful in gaining fee and fame wheresoever he came; villains and savage vikings he slew; the bondes and chapmen (merchants) he left in peace; and he was now a second time called Fridthjof the Bold. He had gotten by this time a large and well-arrayed army, and had become exceedingly rich in chattels. But when Fridthjof had spent three winters in viking expeditions, he sailed west and steered up the Vik (the main part of the present Christiania fjord). Fridthjof said he had a mind to go ashore; 'but you,' said he, 'will have to go a harrying this winter; for I am growing tired of warfare, and I am going to the uplands to find king Ring, and have a talk with him; but you shall come back next summer and get me, and I will be here on the first day of summer.' Said Bjorn: 'This is no wise plan; however, your will must prevail; my wish it would be to go north to Sogn, and kill both the kings Halfdan and Helge.' Made answer Fridthjof: 'That is of no use; I prefer to go and find king Ring and Ingeborg.' Said Bjorn: 'I am unwilling to run the risk of sending you alone into his hands, for although he is somewhat advanced in age, Ring is a wise man and of noble birth. Fridthjof said he must have his own way; and you, Bjorn, said he, will have to be the commander of our company in the meantime.' They did as he would have it. So Fridthjof went to the uplands in the autumn, for he was curious to see the love betwixt king Ring and Ingeborg. Before he came thither he put on a large cowled cloak over the other clothes, all shaggy. He had two staves in his hands, a mask over his face, and made himself look as old as possible. Afterward he met some herd-

at the king's dwelling.' Asked the old man: 'Is Ring a mighty king?' Made answer they: 'To us you seem to be so old a man that you ought to know what manner of man king Ring is in all respects.' The old man said he had been thinking more about salt-boiling than about the manner of kings. After this he went up to the king's hall. Toward the close of the day he went in, assumed a very feeble look, and stopping near the door he pulled the cowl over his head and hid his face. Said then king Ring to Ingeborg: 'There went a man into the hall much larger than other men.' Answered the queen: 'Such are insignificant tidings here.' The king then spoke to the man-servant who stood before the table: 'Go ask the cowl-man who he is, whence he comes, and where his kinsmen dwell.' The swain then ran over the floor to the stranger and said: 'What is your name, my man? or where were you last night? or where are your kinsmen?' Said the cowl-man: 'You ask your questions rapidly, my fellow; but will you be able to understand if I tell you about these things?' 'Certainly I can,' said the swain. Said the cowl-man: 'Thjof (thief) is my name, at Ulf's (wolf's) I spent last night, and in Anger (grief) I am brought up.' The swain hastened before the king, and told him the answers of the stranger.

Said the king: 'You understood admirably, swain. I know the land called Anger; besides, it may be that this man's mind is not at ease. I think he is a wise man, and a man of great worth.' Said the queen: 'This is a remarkable manner of yours to be so eager to talk with every carle that comes here, whosoever he may be; but so far as this man is concerned, I should like to know of what account he is.' Said the king: 'You do not know any better than I do. I see he is a man that thinks more than he talks, and makes good use of his eyes.' Thereupon the king sent a man for him, and the cowled man went to the inner part of the hall before the king; he bent forward somewhat, and greeted the king in a low voice. Said the king: 'What is your name, my large man?' Made answer the cowled man by singing this stave:

FRIDTHJOF (peace-thief) I was called
When I fared with the vikings;
HERTHJOF (war-thief) when
The widows I grieved;
GEIRTHJOF (spear-thief) when I
The barbed shafts threw;
GUNNTHJOF (battle-thief) when I
'Gainst the kings went;
EYTHJOF (isle-thief) when I
The skerries did plunder;
HELTHJOF (death-thief) when I
The babies did toss up;
VALTHJOF (slain-thief) when I
Higher than men was;
But now since then
With salt-boilers about
Have I been wandering;
With needy salt-carles,
Until hither I came.

Said then the king: 'From many things you have taken the thief's (Thjof's) name; but where were you last night? and where

is your home?' Made answer the cowled man: 'In Anger (grief) I am born, my mind urged me hitherward, but my home is nowhere.' Said the king: 'It may be that you have been brought up in sorrow for awhile, but it may also be that you were born in peace. You must, I think, have spent last night in the forest, for there is no bonde near this place named Ulf (wolf); but when you say you have no home, you undoubtedly mean that you think your home of little consequence, since your heart drove you hitherward.' Said Ingeborg now: 'Go thief (Thjof)! get yourself other night-quarters, or betake yourself to the guest-chamber!' Said the king: 'I am now old enough to arrange seats for my guests; come, stranger, put off your cloak and take a seat at my other hand.' Said the queen: 'Yea, in your dotage you are, when you ask beggars to sit down by your side.' Said Thjof: 'It is not becoming, sir; better is that which the queen said; I am more accustomed to be among salt-boilers than to sit by the side of rulers.' Said the king: 'Do as I will it; for I think my will must prevail this time.' Thjof doffed his cloak, under which he was clad in a dark blue kirtle, and had a goodly ring on his hand; a large silver belt was about his waist; down from the belt hung a large purse full of bright silver coins, and a sword was girt to his side; but on his head he wore a large skin cap; his eyes looked dim and his face was all shaggy. Said the king: 'Now I dare say that things look as we would wish to have them; give him, my queen, a good mantle, and such a one as may be becoming to him.' Answered the queen: 'Your will shall prevail, my lord, but I do not like this Thjof (thief) much.' Then a good mantle was given to him, which he donned and sat down in the high seat beside the king. The queen's face blushed red as blood when she saw the goodly ring, but still she was unwilling to converse with him, while the king was exceedingly cheerful, and said: 'A goodly ring you have on your hand, and you must have been boiling salt a long time before you earned it.' Made answer Thjof: 'This is my whole paternal heritage.' Said the king: 'May be you have more than that, but few salt-boilers are your equal; so I think, lest it should be that old age is fast creeping into my eyes.' So Thjof spent the winter here, heartily treated and highly esteemed by all. He was liberal with his fee and cheerful to everybody. The queen seldom talked to him, but the king and he were always happy when they were together.

XII

THE saga tells that king Ring and his queen and a large company once were to go to a feast. Said king Ring then to Thjof: 'Will you go along, or will you stay at home?' He said he would rather go along. Said the king: 'That suits me better.' So they started, and had to cross a frozen lake. Said Thjof to the king: 'Untrustworthy seems to me the ice, and we seem to be going unwarily.' Said the king: 'It is often to be observed that you have much forethought concerning us.' A little while afterward all the ice broke down; then Thjof leaped to the place that was broken, and pulled up the sled and all that were in it. Both the king and the queen were sitting in the sled. All these, together with the horses hitched to the sled, Thjof suddenly pulled up onto the ice, and then said the king: 'That was a right good lift, Thjof; and Fridthjof the Bold,

had he been here, would not have been able to do it with stronger hands; the doughtiest companions are such men as you.' Now they came to the feast, from which we have no tidings, and the king fared home loaded with seemly gifts. Midwinter had passed, and when spring began the weather grew milder, the forests took to blooming, the grass to growing, and the ships were able to glide betwixt the lands.

XIII

IT was one day that the king said to his courtiers: 'I want you to go with me to the woods today, that we may amuse ourselves and see how fair is the country'; and so they did, a large number of men rambled out into the woods with the king. It happened that the king and Fridthjof were both together in the woods, far from the other men. Said the king that he was heavy, and would fain sleep. Answered Thjof: 'Go home, my lord, for that is more becoming to a man of noble estate than to lie out-of-doors.' Said the king: 'I cannot do that.' Then he laid himself down, fell asleep and snored loudly. Thjof sat near him, drew his sword from the sheath and threw it far away from him. A little while afterward the king sat up and said: 'Is it not true, Fridthjof, that many things entered your mind? But you dealt wisely with those thoughts, and henceforth you shall be held in great honour with us. But I knew you immediately the first evening when you came into our hall, and you shall not speedily leave us; and I think a great future lies before you.' Said Fridthjof: 'My lord, you have treated me well and friendly, but now I must soon be off, for my troops are soon coming to meet me, according to a previous arrangement that I have with them.' Therewith they rode home from the woods, and now the king's folk crowded around them. All went home to the hall and drank freely. At the drinking it was made known to all that Fridthjof the Bold had spent the winter there.

XIV

ONE morning early there was a knock at that door of the hall where the king, the queen and many others were sleeping. Asked the king who was calling at the door. Said he who was outside: 'Fridthjof is here. I am now busk and bowne for my departure.' Then the door was opened. In stepped Fridthjof and sang this stave:

> Now must I thank you,
> Bountifully you have feasted
> The feeder of the eagle.
> Bowne am I for departure.
> Ingeborg can I ne'er forget
> While to both of us life is granted.
> Fare she well! and take she
> This costly gift for many kisses.

Therewith he threw the goodly ring to Ingeborg and bade her accept it. The king smiled at this stave and said: 'So, after all, it came to pass that she got more thanks for your winter quarters

than I, and yet she has not been more kind to you than I.' The king then sent his servants for drink and food, saying that they should eat and drink before Fridthjof went away. 'Sit up, queen,' he added, 'and be of good cheer.' She said she had no mind to eat so early. Said king Ring: 'Let us now all eat together,' and so they did. But when they had been drinking awhile said king Ring: 'I wish you might stay here, Fridthjof, for my sons are as yet nothing but children, but I am old and unfit to ward my land, if anybody should seek it for the purpose of harrying. Soon must I be off, my lord' and he sang this stave:

Live, king Ring,
Hale and long!
The highest of kings
'Neath the northern skies!
Guard well, my king, Y
our queen and land.
Nevermore shall meet again
Ingeborg and I.

Sang king Ring then:

Fare not thus from hence,
My Fridthjof! dearest
Son of kings,
So sad in mind!
Your costly gifts
I shall reward

Better far
Than you are aware.

Sang he this too:

Give I the famous
Fridthjof my wife,
And therewith all
That belongs to me.

Interrupted him straightway Fridthjof, and sang:

I will not accept
Those gifts from you,
Lest fatal illness
Threatens my king.

Said the king: 'I should not have given these things to you had I not thought that this was the case; for I am sick, and I wish you to enjoy this in preference to all others, for you are above all men in Norway. I give you a king's name, too; for her brothers, I think, will be less willing than I am to grant honour to you and give you the wife.' Said Fridthjof: 'Accept many thanks from me, my lord, for your kindness, which is more than I could ask or even think; but as to my rank, I will take nothing more than a jarl's name.' Herewith king Ring, taking Fridthjof's hand, gave him the government of the kingdom, which he had ruled over, and jarl's name therewith. Fridthjof was to rule until the sons of king

Ring were old enough to rule their own kingdom. King Ring kept his sick-bed but a short time, and when he died there was great sorrow in his kingdom. A how was raised over him, and, according to his wish, much fee was buried with him. Then Fridthjof made a great feast, which his folk came to. At this feast king Ring's funeral and Ingeborg's and Fridthjof's wedding were celebrated together. Hereafter Fridthjof began to rule this kingdom, and was thought a most excellent man. He and Ingeborg had many children.

XV

THE kings in Sogn, the brothers of Ingeborg, heard these tidings, that Fridthjof had become the ruler of Ring-ric, and that he had married Ingeborg, their sister. Said Helge to Halfdan, his brother, that it was a great shame and an overbold act, that the son of a herser should marry her. So they gathered together much folk and went with them to Ring-ric with a view to slaying Fridthjof and conquering all the kingdom for themselves. When Fridthjof became aware of this he also gathered together folk and said to the queen: 'A new war has come upon our realm, but, whatever the end of it may be, we do not like to see you in low spirits.' Said she: 'It has now come to this, that we must look to you above all others.' Bjorn had then come from the east to aid Fridthjof. They proceeded to battle, and, as he formerly had been wont, Fridthjof was foremost where the danger was the greatest. He and Helge came to a hand-to-hand struggle, and Fridthjof slew king Helge. Then Fridthjof held up the shield of peace, and thus the battle ceased.

Said Fridthjof then to king Halfdan: 'Two important choices are now in your hands, the one that you surrender everything to me, the other that you get your bane like your brother. It is clear that I am stronger than both of you.' Then Halfdan chose to surrender himself and his kingdom to Fridthjof. Now Fridthjof took the rule of the Sogn-fylke, but Halfdan should be herser in Sogn, and pay tribute to Fridthjof as long as he ruled over Ring-ric. The title of king of Sogn was given to Fridthjof from the time when he gave up Ring-ric to the sons of king Ring, and thereupon he added Hordaland by conquest. Fridthjof and Ingeborg had two sons, Gunnthjof and Hunthjof. Both of these became men of might. And now here ends the saga of Fridthjof the Bold.